# Thumbprint Mysteries

# MEASURE ONCE, KILL TWICE

## BY

## KATHLEEN ANNE BARRETT

CB

CONTEMPORARY BOOKS

*a division of* NTC/CONTEMPORARY PUBLISHING GROUP
Lincolnwood, Illinois USA

Thumbprint
Mysteries

# MORE THUMBPRINT MYSTERIES

by Kathleen Anne Barrett:

*A Corpse in the Basement*
*Lethal Delivery, Postage Prepaid*

This is a work of fiction. The characters, incidents, and dialogues are products of the author's imagination and are not to be construed as real. Any resemblance to actual events or persons, living or dead, is entirely coincidental.

Cover Illustration: Ellen Pettengell

ISBN: 0-8092-0644-7

Published by Contemporary Books,
a division of NTC/Contemporary Publishing Group, Inc.,
4255 West Touhy Avenue,
Lincolnwood (Chicago), Illinois 60646-1975 U.S.A.
Manufactured in the United States of America.

890 QB 0 9 8 7 6 5 4 3 2 1

# CHAPTER 1

"Do you remember Mrs. Miller?" Dave asked me. "The old woman who died several months ago in Bob and Sheila's house?"

"Sure," I said. "She died from a diabetic coma, right?"

Dave let out a big sigh. "That's what everybody thinks," he said. "But I think she may have been murdered."

I opened my eyes really wide and stared at him. "Why do you think that?" I said.

Dave sat down at my kitchen table and leaned back in his chair. "Bob and Sheila were in a car accident yesterday. Bob was killed and Sheila's in a coma."

"Oh, my God," I said. "Do they think she'll be all right?"

"I don't know," Dave said. "I have no idea. The police are investigating the accident, though."

"Why would the police be investigating it?" I asked.

"Because the brakes were tampered with," he said.

1

"They think someone arranged for the so-called accident to happen."

"But what does all that have to do with Mrs. Miller?" I asked. "What makes you think she was murdered?"

"I have a lot of reasons," Dave said. "I actually had some suspicions when she died, but they ruled it a natural death so I decided I must be imagining things. Now I'm pretty sure I wasn't."

I was just about to say something when Dave made one of his crazy suggestions. "How would you like to take a shot at solving another murder?" he asked.

My first impulse was to say no. Although we'd just recently solved two murders all on our own, we were hardly trained for the job. Neither of us had had any experience before that. I'd been charged with the murder of someone I'd been dating and we had to prove my innocence. But this was a little different.

"I don't know," I said. "We nearly got ourselves killed the last time. And this time, neither of us has our own future at stake."

Dave gave me a slightly disapproving look, which made me feel a bit guilty. "I really liked Mrs. Miller," he said. "I want to know what happened. No one even suspects that her death was unnatural. If we don't look into it, nobody will."

"But the police are investigating Bob and Sheila's accident. If you're right, wouldn't they discover that Mrs. Miller was murdered too?"

"Not necessarily," Dave said. "And I don't want to take any chances. They're not likely to open up that case just because of my suspicions."

I sighed and looked at the floor. I knew he was right. And I knew we could probably do it if we put our minds to it. I squeezed my eyes shut. "Okay," I said. "I'll do it." *I must be out of my mind*, I thought, as he gave me a big hug.

In case you don't know me, my name is Annie Johnson. I live in Camden, New Jersey, and I've been here the entire thirty-five years of my life. So has Dave Barrio, my best and oldest friend. We went to high school together for a short while. After spending most of our days skipping out of school, we dropped out when we turned sixteen.

We hung out together doing absolutely nothing for about a year, but then Dave's dad got sick and he had to help support his mom and his little sister. He couldn't get a job so he did odd jobs. He mowed lawns and did landscaping, house painting, and repair work. He'd even build things for people, whatever they needed. If he didn't know how to do something, he kept trying until he figured it out. I must say, I was really impressed by him. I had no idea he was that talented. Today, he has his own carpentry business and he's doing really well. I'm really proud of him.

My life didn't go smoothly at first. The state took me away from my mom when I was ten and gave me to my aunt Barb. She says my dad was such a deadbeat that we were better off without him. It was because of my dad that my mom got stuck with me. Aunt Barb says my mom never felt that way but I know she did. She had no money, no job, and no education. And she told me over and over again that she never wanted me. She said that I was the one who ruined her life, as if I'd asked her to have me in the first place. As far as I'm concerned, if you have a child, that child is your responsibility. But my mom didn't see it that way. I really hated her for that. And I hated her the most because no matter how hard I tried, no matter what I did, I couldn't make her love me. The last time I talked to her was over fifteen years ago.

When I was a kid, I swore I'd never grow up to be like my mother. I'd never drink, I'd never quit school, and I'd never go out with jerks like my father. But I became a heavier drinker than my mom had ever been, and I quit school even younger than she did. I also went out with a bunch of guys who treated me so badly they'd probably make my dad look like some kind of an angel.

By the time I was twenty, I was a hopeless alcoholic. One night, when I felt like I was really losing it, I went to see Dave. The next day, he took me to AA. He dragged me there day after day, until I was finally willing to go by myself. It took me over a year to stop wanting a drink. It took another five or six years before I stopped being afraid I'd start up again. Even now, fifteen years later, a trace of the fear is still there. Dave says it's a good fear, though. It's a fear that keeps me sober.

Two years and seven months after my first AA meeting, I got my GED. Then I started making crafts. They were just little things made out of wood with something painted on them. At first, I just sold things at a few local flea markets, but today I sell at flea markets and craft fairs all over New Jersey and Pennsylvania. I also make things, to order, for three different stores in the area. I make a good living and I'm taking care of myself, which is a lot more than I could ever say for my mom. Just last year, I bought my first home in one of my favorite sections of Camden. A short time later, I found a dead body in my basement, and that's how Dave's and my murder-solving career began.

This time, Dave had been hired to do extensive carpentry work in a large house. He has two men working for him, but he was doing this job himself because he liked the house and the variety of work the owners wanted him to do. The other two guys were handling the other work that came in.

The house was owned by Sheila and Bob Miller, and Bob's elderly mother, Mrs. Miller, was living with them. Dave got to know Mrs. Miller pretty well when he was building some wall-to-wall bookcases in the room next to hers. When she died, he was pretty shaken up, so I wasn't all that surprised that he wanted to help clear up the questions surrounding her death.

"Tell me why you suspect that Mrs. Miller was murdered," I said to Dave. "And why were you already suspicious at the time it happened?"

Dave thought for a few moments. "Okay," he said. "You remember I told you she was a diabetic."

"Yeah?"

"Well, it was type I diabetes, which meant she had to have insulin injections all the time, especially before she ate something. But she was always forgetting to give herself the shots, and she'd eat the wrong kinds of food all the time. Even during the time I was working there, she was put in the hospital for it and I know she'd been there at least two or three times before. She'd eat some candy or cookies and go into a coma because she didn't take the insulin. Everyone in her family knew what she was like."

"But I thought she had a nurse," I said. "Wasn't there someone with her every day?"

"Yes," Dave said. "That's the reason the nurse was there. After the second or third time, they decided she needed to be watched. The nurse always made sure she got the right amount of insulin before every meal. The problem is, the nurse was only there during the day. The night she died, she ate some cookies without taking her insulin and went into a coma. She never came out of it."

"Why was the nurse only there during the day?" I asked.

"I think they figured they didn't need her after Mrs. Miller had her dinner," Dave said. "And she'd be asleep all night so there wasn't any point in the nurse being there, I guess."

"Do you know what time the nurse left the night she died?"

"The same time she always left. Six o'clock. I know that because I'm usually still there at that time."

"What time did you leave that night?" I asked.

"It was at least seven-thirty," he said. "I stayed a little later than usual because she was talking to me and I didn't want to cut her off. I had the impression that she was pretty lonely even though she had a lot of family around."

"And she seemed all right when you left?" I said.

"Yeah, she seemed fine. She looked a little tired, but she always did after she'd had her dinner."

"Where did she get the cookies?" I asked.

"From the kitchen," Dave said. "Bob always had them in the house. They were some sort of sugar wafer and he was addicted to them. They always kept them out of sight, but she managed to find them somehow."

"But I thought she had a hard time getting around."

"She did," Dave said. "That was one of the main reasons I suspected something when it happened. She couldn't walk very well, and she certainly wouldn't have been able to climb very easily. Bob claimed he kept the cookies on the top shelf in one of the kitchen cabinets."

"So she'd have to have gotten out of bed, walked into the kitchen, and then climbed on a chair or something to get to them," I said.

"Right," Dave said, "and I just can't see her being able to do that."

"So what do you think happened?" I asked.

"I think someone put them where she could easily reach them," Dave said. "And I have some pretty good ideas about who it might have been."

# CHAPTER 2

The next morning, when Dave went to the Millers' house, I went with him.

"I still can't understand why you're going to keep working on the house," I told him on the way over. "Bob is dead and Sheila's in a coma. They're the ones who hired you."

"I know," Dave said. "But the cabinets aren't finished and Sheila's still alive. I don't think she'd want me to just abandon it. I have my own key and no one's told me to stop. I'm going to keep working until I hear otherwise."

"But you might not even get paid," I said.

Dave gave me a disapproving look. "They already paid me for this part of the project," he said. "And I don't care about that right now, anyway. All I care about is finding out what happened to Mrs. Miller. The best way to do that is to keep working in the house."

I sighed and looked out Dave's truck window. It was

7

early May and the trees were sprouting their pale green buds. The flowers were out and everything looked cheery and bright. But we were going to solve a murder. It wasn't my idea of the best way to spend the day but I didn't want to argue. Dave was already annoyed with me and I didn't want to irritate him any further.

When we arrived, there was a bright red Camaro in the driveway. "It looks like someone's here," I said.

"That's Alicia," Dave said. "She's Bob and Sheila's daughter. Their only child."

I looked over at Dave. He had an uncomfortable expression on his face. "Do you know her very well?" I asked him.

"Not really," he said. "But I do know she's a spoiled brat. This has to be hard to take for anyone, though, and she's not that old. Early twenties, I think."

Dave knocked on the door rather than using his key. When no one had answered after several minutes, he unlocked the door and we walked in. He called Alicia's name but no one responded. I thought I heard a noise and pointed toward the stairway. Dave nodded and we walked on up.

Alicia was in one of the bedrooms, sitting on a bed and staring into space. She was young, as Dave had said, and very pretty. She had shoulder-length brown hair set in soft curls, clear tanned skin, and big brown eyes. Her clothes looked incredibly expensive and she was covered with gold jewelry. She looked up as we came in and gave Dave a weak smile.

"Hi, Alicia," he said in a sad voice. "I'm sorry about your mom and dad."

She nodded without a word.

"I'm sure your mom will be all right," I said. I had no

idea what I was talking about, of course, but it was the only thing I could think of saying.

Alicia seemed to sense my discomfort and she gave me a kind smile. "Thank you," she said.

Dave sat next to her on the bed and took her hand. "How are you doing?" he said. "Do you need anything?"

She shrugged and looked away. "I'm okay," she said.

"I thought I'd just continue working on the cabinets," Dave told her. "I think that's what your mom would want me to do."

Alicia gave Dave a sharp look. "No," she said. "I don't think you should. She wouldn't want to spend the money. It was my father who wanted to waste it all on the house."

Dave frowned. "Alicia," he said, "your mother already paid me to do it. The work's already started and the money's already spent. I'm obligated to finish the job. If I don't, she won't be getting what she paid for."

Alicia looked as if she were about to protest, but she stopped herself. "I suppose you're right," she said. "Mom would want you to finish it. But I don't think you should do anything else after that," she added.

"Okay," Dave said. "They hadn't told me what they wanted done next, anyway."

Alicia stood up and started toward the door, but Dave stopped her. "Alicia," he said, "could I ask you a few questions before you go?"

She stopped, but I saw the tense look on her face. I had the feeling she wasn't in the mood for questions right then, and I was surprised that Dave had asked her. She turned around and looked at him but didn't say a word.

"I just want to ask you what you think about all of this," he said. "I know this is a bad time for you but I have a good reason for not wanting to wait."

Alicia remained where she was and waited for him to continue.

"Someone obviously tampered with your dad's brakes," Dave said, "and I think . . ."

Alicia interrupted him. "I don't think that's true," she said. "That car was really old and I was having trouble with the brakes when I was using it. Don't you remember? You were here when I asked my cousin Joe to look at them."

Dave frowned at Alicia and looked at me. "That's right," he said. "I do remember that. He came with his mother to visit your grandmother. What was his mother's name?"

"Patricia," Alicia said.

"Did he find anything wrong with the brakes?" Dave said.

"He hardly took the time to look," Alicia said. "I told him it was important and that I was afraid something would happen, but all he did was glance under the hood. Then he told me they were fine and walked away."

"How did they work the rest of the day?" Dave said.

"They worked okay for a while and then they'd act funny. The same way they had all day."

"How did they act funny?" Dave said.

Alicia paused for a moment. "Well, sometimes they'd sort of stick," she said. "And then other times they'd take too long to work. I would try to stop at a light and I was afraid they weren't going to work but then they finally would."

"Did you tell your parents about it?" I said.

"Of course," Alicia said. "I just assumed they'd get it taken care of but they obviously didn't. I was using it again when they were in Jamaica, and they still weren't working right."

Dave raised an eyebrow. "Do you know where they usually had the car serviced?" he asked.

"They always had Joe do it," Alicia said. "They liked giving him the business. I guess it made them feel good."

"Do you have any idea when they took it in last?" I asked her.

Alicia gave me a condescending look. "Don't you think I have better things to do than keep track of my parents' car maintenance schedule?" she said.

It took a bit of effort to keep my expression neutral but I managed it somehow.

"Do you have any idea who might want to hurt your parents?" Dave asked her.

"Of course not," she said.

"Alicia," he said in a kind voice, "we're just trying to help you. Do you know if your parents were in any sort of trouble? Did they seem upset about anything or act like they were afraid of something?"

"No. I mean, well, yes. Maybe."

I raised my eyebrows at Dave.

"What do you mean?" Dave asked her.

"They did seem anxious lately," Alicia said. "But they had a lot on their minds. They've never been the same since Grandma died."

Dave gave Alicia a sympathetic look. "They were very close to her, weren't they?" he said.

Alicia nodded.

"And so were you," Dave said.

She nodded again.

"Alicia," Dave said, "I don't know how to tell you this, especially after what's happened to your mom and dad."

She wrinkled her brow as she waited for him to continue.

Dave took a deep breath. "I think your grandmother may have been murdered," he said.

Alicia gasped and moved toward the bed. Dave grabbed her by the elbow and helped her to sit down.

"I'm sorry," he said. "Maybe I shouldn't have told you so soon, but I want to find out who did it. I cared about her and I know you did too. You were the one who paid the most attention to her. I was hoping you could help me."

Alicia looked at him with a mixture of fright, confusion, and sadness. I really felt sorry for her. I wanted to say something comforting but I had the feeling she wouldn't appreciate it coming from me. She didn't know me and hadn't had a chance to warm up to me yet.

She sat in silence for a while and stared at her hands. Dave put his hand on her shoulder and she started to cry. "I don't know what to do," she said. "My whole life is one big nightmare. I don't know what to do."

Dave hugged her close to him and talked to her in a soft voice. "It'll be all right," he said. "We'll find out who did this. Don't you worry. Annie and I have solved murders before. We'll do it again. We'll find out who's doing this to your family, but we need your help. Do you think you can do it?" he asked.

"Yes," she said. "I'll help you in any way I can."

# CHAPTER 3

I spent the next half-hour looking around Bob and Sheila's house while Dave went to work on the new kitchen cabinets he was constructing. I felt a little uncomfortable snooping but not uncomfortable enough to stop. I went through every one of the four bedrooms. I was trying to get an idea of what Bob and Sheila were like. The master bedroom was enormous. The French doors were covered with heavy brocade curtains and the spread on the king-sized bed was made of satin. Everything was red and gold. It was pretty gaudy, if you want the truth.

After I went through the other three bedrooms and found nothing that interested me, I went back downstairs. I found the room with the floor-to-ceiling bookcases Dave had told me about. There was a big wooden desk in the center of the room with a very neat surface. Nothing was on it but a letter opener, a pair of scissors, a pen set, and a Rolodex file with names, phone numbers, and addresses. I looked through the file and noticed a lot of names I recognized. I found a sheet of paper in one of the drawers and copied their numbers and addresses. I put the paper in my back pocket and left the room.

I knew that the room next door to the study was the one Mrs. Miller had stayed in. I opened the door and peeked in with a nervous knot in my stomach. I don't know what I was afraid of. I think it was just the idea that she had died there, and I was pretty sure she'd been murdered. It made me feel a little creepy.

The room smelled musty and was nearly empty. There was a hospital-type bed in the center of the room, stripped to the bare mattress. It made me think of those movies where someone comes to a hospital room to see a loved one and there's nothing there but an empty bed. There's a woman cleaning the room with the drapes pulled wide open to let in the sun. The visitor asks about the patient who'd been there and is told that she died during the night. I shuddered and looked away.

There were several cardboard boxes on the floor and a few dresses in the closet. The dresses were an old-fashioned style, like the housedresses my own grandmother used to wear. I didn't think they made them anymore.

I looked inside the boxes. There were no papers of any kind but I found a Bible, a rosary, and a prayer book. I opened the Bible where she'd marked it with the ribbon. Psalm 23. I read the psalm and closed the book. Tears filled my eyes and I was trying to shake the feeling when Dave walked in.

"What are you doing?" he said. "I thought you were going to sit in the kitchen with me."

I wiped a tear from my cheek and he frowned. "You're

too sensitive," he said. "Don't let it get to you. You didn't even know her."

"I can't help it," I said. "It's just the way I am."

He gave me a half-understanding, half-amused smile. "Come on," he said. "I want to talk to you."

"What did Bob do for a living?" I asked Dave when we sat down at the kitchen table.

"He was a truck driver," Dave said. When he saw my frown, he said, "Mrs. Miller gave them a lot of money to fix up the house. She didn't want him to have to wait until she died. She wanted to see him enjoy it. He'd always wanted to fix up the house so she gave him whatever he needed to do it. They went all out, but they were happy and so was she. Some of it's a bit overdone but that was Sheila's taste."

I laughed. "The master bedroom looks like one of those brothels in an old western movie," I said.

"To each his own," Dave said.

"What did Sheila do?" I asked.

"She's a nurse at Our Lady of Lourdes," he said.

I wrinkled my brow. "A nurse?" I said. "Then why did they have to hire another one to take care of Mrs. Miller?"

"Because Sheila had her own job," Dave said. "She didn't have time to work her own shifts and take care of Mrs. Miller too."

I had a sudden thought. "Weren't Sheila and Bob here the night Mrs. Miller died?" I asked. "Wouldn't they have heard her moving around? And why wouldn't Sheila give her a shot of insulin after she ate the cookies?"

"Because they weren't here," Dave said. "They were in Hawaii on vacation."

"So it was unusual for her to be all alone in the house," I said.

"Well, not exactly," Dave said. "Bob and Sheila took a lot of vacations. They were in Jamaica just last week. They were only back two days before the accident happened. They were on their way to church. The whole family is pretty religious, I think."

"Yeah, I saw Mrs. Miller's Bible and things."

"She really missed going to church with Bob and Sheila," Dave said. "But she watched the mass on TV every morning. She used to go to church every day before her legs got bad."

"So how are we going to handle this investigation?" I said. "Who do we have that we can talk to besides Alicia?"

"Well, there's Alicia's cousin, Joe, and Joe's mom, Patricia. She was Mrs. Miller's daughter but I don't think they saw much of each other."

"Did Mrs. Miller have any other children?"

"She had another son but he died years ago in a car accident."

My antennae went up. "How many years ago?" I said with a suspicious look on my face.

Dave gave me a patient smile. "About twenty," he said. "No connection. Trust me."

I shrugged. "Anyone else?"

"Just Angie," Dave said.

"Who's Angie?"

"The nurse who took care of Mrs. Miller. She was the daughter of the son who died."

My eyes bugged out. "You mean the nurse was related to Mrs. Miller?" I said.

"Yeah, she was her granddaughter," Dave said in a matter-of-fact voice.

"Don't you think this is a little weird?" I said.

"What?" Dave said.

"That Sheila is a nurse, that the nurse who took care of Mrs. Miller was her granddaughter, but that no one was here when she died."

Dave looked at me like I had a screw loose. "What's your point?" he said. "Bob and Sheila were on vacation. That wasn't the least bit unusual for them. And Angie always went home at six o'clock. That was her regular routine. Why do you find that so strange?"

"I don't know," I said. "But something about it doesn't feel right."

"No kidding," Dave said. "That's what I've been trying to tell you. It didn't feel right to me when it happened, and now I'm more suspicious than ever. I really think one of them killed her."

"But who would do it, and why? What motive could they have?"

"Money," Dave said. "She had an awful lot of it."

"Do you know if she had a will?"

"I'm sure she did," he said. "I heard her talking about it."

"You heard her talking about her will?" I said. "What did she say?"

"I didn't hear the whole conversation," Dave said. "I wasn't in the study at the time. I was in the bathroom. But she was angry and she was yelling pretty loud. It was the day that Patricia and Joe were here with Alicia. That was when I got the impression that Joe and Patricia hadn't seen much of her over the years. She was screaming at them to get out. She said something about them coming to see her only because she was old and they thought she was dying. She was telling them she was going to live another ten years. Then she told them she was going to take them out of her will for being so greedy and selfish."

"Are you sure you know who she was talking to?" I said.

"I assumed she was talking to Patricia and Joe," Dave said. "She said they never came to see her until now that she was old. She thought they were suddenly pretending to care about her because they wanted her money. I don't see how she could have been talking to Alicia. She was here all the time. And she couldn't have been talking to Angie, either. Angie had been here for months, and she was always very kind and patient with Mrs. Miller. She wasn't accepting any money for taking care of her, either. I heard Mrs. Miller insist she let her pay her but Angie always refused. She couldn't have been talking to Angie or Alicia. It had to have been Joe and Patricia."

"Do you think it was true that they hadn't seen her in all that time?" I said. "Had you ever seen them before?"

"That was the only time I saw them," Dave said.

"How soon after that did she die?" I asked.

"The same night," Dave said. "That was the night she ate the cookies."

# CHAPTER 4

The next day I had a craft show to do and Dave spent the day at the Miller house. We met at seven o'clock for dinner in a little restaurant on the west side of town. It's one of my favorite places to eat. There's no sign on the outside so if you don't already know it's there, you'd never stop in. I keep telling Fran, the owner, that a sign might bring in more business, but she says she doesn't want any more.

"I like things just as now," she says in her Armenian accent. "Simple is good. Too many people make me nervous."

We ordered our usual, an Italian sort of dish made with pasta, hot sauce, and a lot of vegetables and grilled chicken. Fran doesn't cook Armenian. She says it reminds her too much of home.

"I have a plan," Dave said after Fran served us our food.

I raised an eyebrow. "So let's hear it," I said.

"First, we talk to Angie. She spent the most time with Mrs. Miller, and I know she cared about her. She was really kind to her grandmother."

"Do you know where she lives?" I asked.

"We'll find out," he said. "I'm sure she'll be at Bob's viewing tomorrow."

"Okay. So what's the rest of the plan?"

Dave swallowed a mouthful of food. "We talk to Joe and Patricia," he said as if he'd given it a great deal of thought.

"Wow, that's quite a plan," I said. "What do we do if they don't know anything?"

Dave was about to give me a dirty look when he saw the smile on my face. "I know it's not much," he said. "But it's all I have for now. Do you have any better ideas?"

"Well," I said, "what I'd really like to do is get a look at Mrs. Miller's will."

"How do you suggest we do that?" he said. "I doubt if anyone would show it to us."

"I doubt it too," I said. "Especially if they were named as a beneficiary."

"I wonder if she really took Patricia out?" Dave said.

"I don't see how she'd have had the time," I said. "She died the same night she threatened to change the will."

We looked at each other for a few moments. "It sure makes them pretty strong suspects, doesn't it?" Dave said.

"Yeah, but it's almost too obvious," I said. "It can't be that easy. And it is possible that she changed the will. She could have had Alicia and Angie witness it. All she'd have to do is scribble something on a piece of paper. I don't think it has to be typed."

"Well, we'll have to ask them, won't we?"

"Is this an addition to the plan?" I asked him with a teasing smile.

"Most definitely," he said with a smile back.

"I wonder how much money she really had," I said. "Do you have any idea?"

Dave shook his head. "No, but I know it was a lot. I heard Bob and Sheila talking one day. Sheila was telling him she didn't want to spend all of the money on the house and Bob told her not to worry. He said there was enough to do whatever they wanted for the rest of their lives. All they had to do was wait."

I stared at Dave with my mouth open. "I can't believe he said that," I said. "She was being so generous with him. She was giving him all the money he wanted, and she was doing it before she died so he wouldn't *have* to wait. What more could he ask for?"

Dave laughed. "I guess he wanted it all," he said. "When people get greedy, there's no satisfying them. They just want more and more and they want it yesterday."

I didn't answer. I was thinking and I had a frown on my face.

"What's the matter?" Dave said.

"You don't think Bob and Sheila could have killed her, do you?" I asked.

Dave stared off into space for several moments. "I suppose they could have," he said slowly. "But then who tried to kill Bob and Sheila?"

"Maybe Bob did it. Or Sheila."

"Huh?" Dave said. He looked at me like I was crazy. "That's totally ridiculous."

"Well, just hear me out," I said. "Think about it. Bob and Sheila were inheriting most of the money, right?"

"We don't have any way of knowing that," Dave said. "Patricia and Joe and Angie could have gotten some too. Or Alicia. And maybe there are other relatives we don't even know about."

"Okay, fine," I said. "We'll have to find that out. But we do know that Bob and Sheila already had been given a lot of money, right?"

"Yes, so what's your point?"

"So maybe either Bob or Sheila wanted all that money for himself or herself."

Dave gave me one of those looks that make me feel two feet tall.

"Just listen," I said. "It's not as stupid as you think."

He rolled his eyes but he let me continue.

"What if Bob was cheating on Sheila, for example?" I said. "He has a girlfriend and he wants to run off with her and take all the money. So he plans an accident, thinking he'll jump out and Sheila will be killed. Only it doesn't work out and he gets killed instead."

Dave shook his head and looked away. "Are you serious?" he said when he looked back at me. "Because if you are, I'm getting myself a new partner."

I could feel my face turn red. "Or," I said, not knowing when to quit, "maybe Sheila planned the accident to kill Bob so *she* could have all the money. Bob gets killed and she survives."

"Do you think she planned the part about the coma too?" Dave asked.

"No," I said with the little patience I had left. "But she may come out of it. You never know."

Dave looked skyward and stopped talking.

"Do you have any better ideas?" I said.

"No," he said. "Actually, your theories aren't completely ridiculous."

I stared at him with my mouth open.

"But they only make sense if we assume that Bob and Sheila are two of the stupidest people on the face of the earth."

That time I burst out laughing. "Yeah, I guess you're right," I said. "It'd be too risky. They live on that steep hill and they'd have to know they'd be picking up speed every second. It's a miracle either of them survived. But whoever did it can't be too smart. They tampered with the brakes in a way that no one could miss. There was no way anyone was going to think it was an accident. And since that's the case, the only possible intelligent reason for doing it would be to throw the police off the track."

Dave frowned and watched me for several moments. "Off the track of *what*?" he said with a look of genuine concern.

I let out a heavy sigh. "I don't know," I said. "I think I'm just tired. Even I'm starting to realize that I'm not making any sense."

Dave looked relieved and patted me on the arm. "Forget about it," he said. "We'll talk about it later."

"Well, I still think Bob or Sheila could have killed Mrs. Miller, though," I said. "I don't trust either of them."

"Why not?" Dave said.

"Because of what you heard them say about the money," I said. "And because Sheila's a nurse."

"Who cares if she's a nurse?" Dave said. "What's that got to do with anything?"

"Because she'd know all about Mrs. Miller's diabetes and what it would take to kill her. She'd know exactly what to do."

"Then Angie would be in the same position," Dave said. "She's a nurse too."

I thought about that for a moment. "You're right," I said. "And Angie was the one who spent the most time with Mrs. Miller. She knew more about her condition than anyone."

"Everyone knew about her condition," Dave said. "You have to remember that. There wasn't a person in that family that didn't know what she needed and the problems she got herself into. It could be any one of them. Hell, it could even be one of the other workers they've had in the house."

I wrinkled my brow. "There were other workers?" I said. "When?"

"On and off the whole time I've been there," Dave said. "They weren't just having carpentry work done. They did all three of the bathrooms and a big part of the basement."

"Do you know who these people are?" I said.

"I could probably find most of them," he said. "I know the companies they work for."

We didn't have to work that hard. Two of those same workers were at the viewing the next night.

# CHAPTER
# 5

The next day, I was so
nervous about attending Bob's viewing that I couldn't
think straight. I know it didn't make any sense, but it had
been a while since our first murder investigation. I wasn't
sure I could do it again. And I was nervous about who
might show up. I've read that murderers often attend the
viewings and funerals of their victims, sort of like people
who watch a fire they've set.

I spent the day painting and puttering, trying different
stencils on the same object over and over again. I must
have done one little step stool eight different times. It
wasn't intentional. I just kept making mistakes.

When it came time to get ready for the viewing, I
couldn't calm myself down. I knew I needed to eat
something, but I just didn't have an appetite. I couldn't
decide what to wear. It was ninety degrees outside and I
don't own any summer dresses in black or gray. I chose
white instead and hoped no one would care.

Dave picked me up at six-thirty. He was wearing a red T-shirt and jeans. I gave him a big grin and felt really glad to be with him. He was either someone with his priorities straight or he didn't own anything black, either.

The first person we saw when we got there was Alicia. She was dressed in a spaghetti-strap black cocktail dress. I don't want to dwell so much on the fashion aspect of viewings, but it was kind of funny. Dave gave her a hug and I offered her my hand. Her face and eyes were quite red and most of her makeup was gone. "I'm sorry, Alicia," I said. What else do you say to someone at a time like that? She gave me a sad little smile.

After we moved away from Alicia, I asked Dave if Patricia and Joe or Angie were there. He looked around the room. A few moments later, he put up his hand and waved to someone. I looked across the room and saw a woman return his wave with a slight smile.

"Come on," Dave said to me. "That's Angie."

Dave introduced me to a young woman who was very thin and quite tall. Her blond hair was cut close to her head and slicked back with gel.

"How you holding up, Angie?" Dave asked in a consoling voice.

"As well as I can. I was just at the hospital to see Sheila. It's probably better she can't be here to see this. On the other hand, can you imagine the trauma of waking up to be told that your husband's dead and buried?"

I shuddered. "Has there been any change in her condition?" I said.

Angie shook her head. "Not a bit," she said.

"Do they expect her to wake up?"

"They just don't know. You can't tell with something like this. You just have to wait and see what happens."

"Have you seen Patricia and Joe?" Dave asked her.

"Not yet," she said. "I'm expecting them to be late, though. They were out of town when they heard the news."

"Where were they?" Dave asked.

"I don't know," she said. "You'll have to ask Alicia. She's the one who phoned them."

Something occurred to me just then. I wasn't sure it was the right time but I decided to ask anyway. "Did Mrs. Miller have any other relatives besides you, Patricia and Joe, Bob and Sheila, and Alicia?" I said.

"Not on this side of the family," Angie said, "but my grandfather had a brother."

I was trying to get the family straight in my head. "So Mrs. Miller was your grandmother and Alicia's grandmother."

"Right," Angie said. "And she was also Joe's grandmother."

"And she was Bob's mother and Patricia's mother."

"Yes, and she was also my father's mother, but he died in a car accident shortly after I was born."

"And then your grandfather, who was Mrs. Miller's husband, had a brother."

Angie nodded. "Yeah. His name was Frederick."

"Is he dead?" I asked.

"Well, I'm not really sure," Angie said. "He was one of those wanderer types. We'd see him every once in a while. He never seemed to have a job but he always managed to survive. He'd show up and stay with us for a month or two, and then he'd take off in the middle of the night without even saying good-bye. It was weird. I was so young I can barely remember him. Grandma claimed she heard from him from time to time, but I always thought she was just telling me stories."

"I hope you don't think this is too personal," I said,

"but did your grandmother's money come from her side of the family or from your grandfather's?"

"It came from my grandfather," Angie said.

"Isn't that Joe and Patricia?" Dave said to Angie.

Angie looked toward the door. "Yes," she said. "Come on, Annie. I'll introduce you."

Patricia was middle-aged, thin like Angie, and also quite tall. Joseph was at least six-two with wavy brown hair. He was very polite and friendly, and I liked him right away.

"How's Alicia holding up?" Patricia asked Angie after we were introduced.

"She's having a hard time of it," Angie said. "She was crying so hard when I got here I could barely control her. I didn't know what to do. I finally went across the street and got her a cup of coffee with a shot of whiskey in it. It seemed to help a little."

I glanced over at Alicia. She was standing near the door, allowing the guests to console her as they came in. She seemed so fragile in the black dress. She was the only one in the family who wasn't tall, and it made her seem all the more vulnerable. I looked away.

Dave was looking across the room and squinting as if he were trying to recognize someone.

"What are you staring at?" I whispered to him.

"Come on," he said. "I think I see two of the guys who did the tile work on the bathrooms in the house."

As we got closer to the men Dave had been watching, a look of recognition swept over his face and he grinned at the two men.

"Hey, Gus and Gerry. How's it going?" Dave said. "This is Annie Johnson, a close friend of mine."

When they started grinning and teasing him, Dave

gave the old guy a punch in the arm. "Cut it out, Gus. Annie's just a friend. You know about Marla. I'm still with her."

I felt the blood rise to my face and I looked down, hoping no one would notice.

"I didn't know you were that close to the Millers," Gus said to Dave. "Didn't expect to see you here. It's a nice surprise. You still working over at the house?"

"Yeah, I'm doing some kitchen cabinets now and they'll probably take a while. Sheila already paid for them so I figured I should keep on going."

"What do you think of all this?" Gerry said. "Do you really think someone tried to kill them?"

"It sure looks that way," Dave said. "The brake line was punctured and whoever did it knew they'd be going down that steep hill. I still can't believe Sheila survived it."

Gus shook his head. "It's a sad world, ain't it?" he said. "And what a sad state of affairs for that family. First the old woman and now those two." He shook his head again and stared at his feet.

"Did either of you guys ever hear anything while you were at the house?" Dave asked.

"Like what?" Gerry said.

"Anything that didn't sound right. Did you ever overhear anyone say something that just didn't sit right with you?"

Gus was frowning and shaking his head. Gerry just frowned and pursed his lips. "The only thing I can think of is I didn't like the way that girl, Alicia, talked to her mother sometimes. It just wasn't respectful," Gerry said.

"What did you hear her say?" I asked.

"I can't even remember," he said. "I just remember I didn't like it."

"Did she ever threaten her or anything like that?" Dave said.

"No, it was nothing like that," Gerry said. "Just disrespectful, that's all."

"Was there anything else that you witnessed while you were working there that you thought was suspicious in any way?" Dave said.

Gerry frowned. "No, of course not. Why are you asking all these questions?"

"No reason," Dave said. "Just curious."

On the ride home, I said, "So what did you think about what Gerry said—about the way Alicia talked to Sheila?"

Dave turned and looked at me. "What's the big deal?" he said. "Sheila is Alicia's mother and Alicia's a spoiled brat. It's just normal mother-daughter stuff."

"Yeah, you're probably right," I said. Then I grinned. "I couldn't get over that old guy, Gus. I can't believe he's still working."

Dave laughed. "I don't think he's anywhere near as old as you think. He just looks old because he lost all his teeth."

I laughed even harder than Dave. "So, Mr. Detective, what's next on the agenda?"

"I'd like to talk to Joe or Patricia," he said. "Your choice."

I thought for a few moments. "Patricia," I said. "I think I'd really like to talk to Patricia."

# CHAPTER 6

The funeral was the next morning. Dave picked me up early and took me out to breakfast, which was a nice treat. We went to Sal's, where they serve everything from corned beef hash (which I like well enough) to chipped beef on toast (which I wouldn't eat unless it was the only food on earth). Dave ordered the chipped beef and I nearly gagged watching him eat it.

"Did you think anyone acted suspicious at the viewing last night?" I asked him.

Dave thought for a few moments. "No. At least I didn't notice anything. Why? Did you?"

"Everyone seemed to be acting pretty much the way I'd expect them to act," I said. Then I frowned. "Did you notice any police there?"

"No, but how would I know who they were?"

"Usually those guys stick out like a sore thumb," I said.

"We'll keep a lookout today," he said.

"And we should also watch for the mysterious brother," I added.

Dave wrinkled his brow. "The what?"

"Frederick. Mr. Miller's long-lost brother," I said. "The one Angie was telling us about."

Dave shook his head at me. "Do you really think some guy that no one's seen for something like twenty years is going to show up at Bob's funeral and then not even identify himself?" he said.

"Why not?" I said. "Maybe Mrs. Miller's lawyers hired someone to find him when she died," I said. "If he was named in the will, they'd have to look for him, wouldn't they?"

"I don't know," Dave said. "I guess so. But I doubt that they have to go to that much trouble."

"Well, I still think it's a possibility and we shouldn't ignore it," I said stubbornly.

Dave smiled. "What do you want to talk to Patricia about?" he said. "Do you have something special in mind?"

"Mostly I just want to know why she hadn't seen her mother in all those years. I want to know what happened between them. Do you know how long it had been since they'd seen each other?"

Dave shook his head with his mouth full of food. "No," he said a few moments later. "But I got the impression it was pretty long from the way everybody acted the day they came."

"How did they act?" I said.

"Well, first of all, Mrs. Miller didn't even recognize Joseph. I heard her ask who he was."

"Yeah, but that could just be because he was a kid the

last time she saw him. You know how fast kids change when they're growing up. It wouldn't have to be that many years for him to look unfamiliar."

"I guess you're right," Dave said. "But there was more to it than that. Mrs. Miller really seemed shocked to see them."

"I wonder why they came when they did?" I said.

"Yeah, I wonder too. Funny how she just happened to die that very same night. If you ask me, it's too much of a coincidence."

I agreed and looked at my watch. It was funeral time. Dave paid the bill and we drove to the church in almost complete silence. I was trying to sort out what I'd learned so far to see if any of it made any sense. So far, it really didn't.

When we arrived at the church, we had a hard time finding a parking spot. There was no lot to speak of so almost everyone had to park on the street.

The funeral was well attended. Apparently, Bob had a lot of friends who hadn't shown up at the viewing. I thought about Sheila only a few miles away in a hospital bed, totally unaware that any of this was going on. The idea of being in a coma has always been fascinating to me, as well as very strange. I wondered how much of what was happening she *really* knew.

The service was short. Angie gave a eulogy that was very nice but not overly emotional. I was grateful for that. I'd never even met Bob, but I don't like to watch other people's pain. I would have made a terrible psychologist or doctor.

I looked around the church throughout the service. I think I was really looking for the missing relative more than anyone, but I was also looking for guilty faces. I didn't see even one. Everyone who'd been at the viewing was at the funeral, plus at least two dozen more.

"Who do you think all these extra people are?" I asked Dave when we were standing on the steps after the service.

"What do you mean by extra people?" he asked with a frown.

"Well, there are so many here that weren't there last night."

Dave looked around. "Some of them worked at the house," he said. "Maybe some of the others were co-workers."

"Do you think we should ask some of them?" I said.

"Why not?" he said. "Come on."

Dave grabbed my hand and I just followed his lead. We walked toward a group of men who were talking rather loudly just outside the door.

"Excuse me," Dave said as he held his hand out to one of the men. The man took Dave's hand easily and shook it. After they'd all exchanged handshakes, Dave introduced me and asked if they'd mind if we asked them a few questions. Each one seemed undisturbed by the idea.

"I don't know if you know this," Dave said, "but the police are sure that Bob's death wasn't an accident. They know the brakes were tampered with. I worked for the Millers. In fact, I still do, and I'm trying to find out what happened."

All four men were listening intently. When Dave said we were trying to find out what happened, eight eyebrows went up at once.

"How did you guys know Bob?" Dave said next.

"We worked with him," one of the men said. He was

about five-feet-five with a heavy brown beard and over-developed arm muscles.

"Did you know him well?" Dave asked.

"You don't really get to know people too well in this business," another of them said. "We're out on the road most of the time so we don't get too much chance to mingle, if you know what I mean."

"Did any of you ever have any real conversations with him?" I asked.

They all turned to look at me. "I did," said a tall guy with thinning black hair and a great build. "We went out for a drink or two once in a while. I was going through a divorce a while back and I needed a shoulder to cry on. Bob was a good listener."

I smiled. "Did he ever talk about himself?" I asked.

The man looked almost guilty. "Not much," he said. "He mostly just listened like I told you. I guess I hogged most of the conversation."

I gave him an understanding look. "There's nothing wrong with that," I said. The man smiled at me and then began to stare at me in such a way that my alarm buttons started going off. I turned to the other three men.

"How about you guys? Did any one of you ever really get to talk to him?"

They looked at each other and started shifting their feet.

"The reason I'm asking," I said, "is that I want to know if he ever said anything about being afraid of anyone. Or if he ever talked about being in any kind of trouble."

They looked from one to the other and all shook their heads. "Sorry," the short, muscled man said. "I can't help you. He never said anything like that to me."

"Me either," said the black-haired guy. The other two agreed.

We thanked them for their time and left. Then Dave steered me toward a couple of guys on the lawn.

"Just let me do the talking," he said to me. "These guys worked at the house a while back but they were always getting into spats with the Millers. Bob ended up firing them both. I heard the company they worked for then fired them after Bob wrote the company a letter."

# CHAPTER 7

"Hey, what are you guys doing here?" Dave said to the two men as we approached them. "You weren't exactly on friendly terms with Bob last time I saw you. Isn't it a little strange, you showing up at his funeral? Last I heard, he got you both fired."

They both muttered the same phrase at Dave and gave me a cold stare. "That's exactly why we're here," one of them said with a voice full of hate. "We wanted a chance to spit on his grave. Neither of us has been able to find work since."

"Is that right?" Dave said. "Then maybe that gives you a pretty good motive for his murder."

Both men laughed unkindly. "I wish I had done it," one of them said. "He got what he deserved. Probably some other poor sucker whose life he screwed up did him in. But it wasn't me and it wasn't Tony, so you're wasting your breath. Now get lost before we put you in the ground with him."

I pulled on Dave's sleeve. "Come on," I said. "Let's get out of here."

"Those guys didn't do it," I said when we were out of their hearing distance.

Dave stared at me. "What makes you say that?" he asked.

"Because they'd be giving too much away by everything they said. They're not even trying to hide the fact that they hated him. They openly admit it. I think if they were guilty, they'd have stayed away altogether."

Dave sighed and turned down his mouth. "Yeah, you're probably right," he said.

"Are there any other people here who worked on the house?"

Dave looked around carefully. "I don't see anyone else," he said. "I wouldn't normally expect them to come anyway. It's not like they were friends with him."

"Well, *you're* here and you're trying to solve his murder," I said.

"That's because of Mrs. Miller," Dave said. "If it wasn't for her, I probably wouldn't be getting myself involved in all this."

I gave him a warm smile. "Let's go find Patricia," I said. "Maybe we can arrange a time to meet with her."

We found Patricia on the lawn on the other side of the church, standing under a big oak tree, talking to Joseph. When we approached, they both gave us somewhat friendly but uncomfortable looks.

Dave held out his hand to Joe, and I smiled at both of them. I felt awkward but there was no way around it. Funerals are always awkward.

"We were wondering if we could come and talk to you sometime," I said quietly to Patricia. "We won't take much of your time. We just want to ask you a few questions."

Patricia gave me a wary look. "What is it you want to talk about?" she asked me. "And why can't you do it now?"

"We could do it now," I said, "if that's all right with you, but I don't think this is the right place. It may also not be a good time for you. I'm sure you want time to recover from all this."

"I don't need to recover from anything," she said with a wave of her hand. "I wasn't close to Bob or Sheila."

I didn't want to reveal my reaction to that, so I just ignored what she said. "The reason we want to talk to you," I said, "is that we think that your mother may have been murdered too."

Patricia gasped and Joe suddenly turned to look at me. "What did you say?" he asked me.

I repeated myself and Dave gave me a warning frown.

"Where would you get such an idea?" Patricia asked. She seemed quite upset but I wasn't sure if it was real or not. Given the strength of their relationship, I couldn't see why the notion of her mother's murder would bother her so much.

"We'll tell you that when we talk," Dave said. "This really isn't the place."

"I'd like to be there too, if you don't mind," Joe said. His voice and expression betrayed his anger.

"We want to talk to both of you," Dave said, "but I'd rather we see you separately."

"Oh, now, wait a minute," Patricia said. "What do you think this is, and who do you people think you are? We don't have to talk to you at all if we don't want to. Come on, Joe."

She and Joe started to walk away and I realized we'd gone too far. I ran after her and motioned for Dave to stay behind.

"Wait," I said as I caught up to them. "I'm really sorry we came off that way. And you're right. You don't have to talk to us."

Patricia stopped walking at that point and looked at me. Joe kept going and she called after him to stop. When he turned around, she motioned for him to come back. He looked at the ground as he walked but he came back.

"I'm really sorry," I said again. "I know you don't have to talk to us, but no one believes that her death was a murder and Dave is pretty sure it was. He was even suspicious about it when it happened, but he decided he was wrong when they ruled it a natural death."

Patricia raised her shoulders and let them drop. Then she looked across the parking lot with an annoyed expression. When she looked back at me, the expression was still on her face.

"I still don't understand what you want from me," she said. "And I don't believe she was murdered, by the way. Why would anyone want to kill her?"

"Money," I said.

"But we were all named in the will," Patricia said.

"That's precisely my point," I said. "Or part of it, anyway. If one of you needed the money really badly and couldn't afford to wait, it might be a reason for murder."

Patricia frowned. "I guess I see what you mean," she said. "But why would any of us need money that badly?"

"That's one of the million-dollar questions," I said. "Do you know if any of the beneficiaries was in financial trouble?"

Patricia wrinkled her brow and Joe started shuffling his feet. "No," she said quickly. Then she looked at Joe. "We really have to be going," she said. "I'm sorry, but we're late already."

She started to walk away and Joe hurried after her.

"When can I talk to you?" I yelled.

She turned around but kept walking. "Ask Alicia for my telephone number and call me," she said.

I went back to the church to find Dave and, hopefully, Alicia. I saw Alicia first.

"Alicia?" I said quietly as I walked over to her. "Can I talk to you for a minute?"

She looked a little bothered by my request but she said yes in a small voice.

"I just wanted to get Patricia's phone number from you," I said. "She told me to ask you."

I had already gotten Patricia's number and address from Bob and Sheila's Rolodex, but I wanted to see how well Alicia knew it. Alicia recited the number by heart. I dug in my purse for a pen and scrap of paper and asked her to repeat it.

"Is that all you want?" she said then. Her face and voice were so sad that I wanted to hug her. I didn't know her that well, though, and I had the feeling she didn't trust me anyway.

"That's it for now," I said with a kind smile.

She gave me a weak smile back and walked away. I put the scrap of paper with the number in my purse and started searching for Dave. It took me awhile to find him, but I finally spotted him halfway behind the tree with Gerry and Gus.

When they saw me walking toward them, both Gerry and Gus smiled.

"Where've you been?" Dave said to me.

"Just talking to Patricia and Alicia," I said.

Then I looked at Gus and Gerry. "Hi," I said, and they said hi back. "Looks like everyone's starting to take off."

Gus looked around. "Yeah," he said. "Guess we'll be going too."

We all exchanged uncomfortable glances and then said good-bye.

# CHAPTER 8

I got up late the next morning and made myself some corn muffins for breakfast. I had a bigger appetite than usual and corn muffins are comfort food to me. I don't know why I felt the need for comfort, but I did. Maybe it was the funeral and all those sad faces. I don't like uncertainty, either, and there's an awful lot of uncertainty involved when you're trying to solve a murder.

At ten o'clock I called Patricia at the number Alicia had given me. All I got was an answering machine. I decided not to leave a message. Then I called Dave at the Millers' house and asked if he had Alicia's number.

"No," he said, "but she's right here. What's up?"

"I just want to ask her for Patricia's work number," I said. "The one she gave me was for her house and she's not there."

"Okay," Dave said and handed Alicia the phone.

When I asked Alicia the number, she said she didn't know it but that Patricia worked at Petite Sophisticate, one of the women's clothing stores in the Deptford Mall. Then she asked why I was so interested in Patricia.

"I'm not any more interested in Patricia than anyone else," I said. "I just want to talk to her and see if she has any information that might help us."

When Alicia just sighed, I said, "How are you feeling today?"

"Okay," she said, sounding as if she appreciated my asking.

"I'm glad," I said and let it go at that. I didn't want to push it. If I started slowly, I thought maybe she'd eventually learn to trust me a little.

After I hung up, I called information and got the number for the clothing store. When I asked for Patricia, the woman who answered made a little huffing sound. Then I heard her cup her hand over the receiver and say something to Patricia about personal calls.

"I'm really sorry for calling you at work," I told Patricia after I identified myself. "I hope I didn't get you in any trouble."

"I really can't talk now," Patricia said nervously.

"Can you talk tonight?" I said. "Your place or mine?"

She sighed loudly and rattled off her address. "I get off at six. Come anytime after seven." Then she hung up.

I called Dave right back and asked if he wanted to come with me. "Sure thing," he said. "I'll see you at your place at six-thirty."

I got out my paint supplies and a wooden plaque and set to work. I'd been making wall plaques for children's rooms that said "Now I Lay Me Down to

Sleep" and they'd been selling really well. I was right in the middle of painting the word *Sleep* when I got an idea. I closed up my paints, cleaned off the brushes, and called the hospital where Sheila was staying. They gave me the visiting hours but told me that only family members were allowed. I said I was a niece and the nurse said that was fine. I almost called Dave again but decided not to. He was working and Alicia was there. I really didn't want Alicia to know what I was doing.

When I got to the hospital, I signed the register so that no one could possibly read my name. Then I went to Sheila's room and poked my head around the corner to make sure no one else was there. I sat next to her bed and held her hand. Then I started talking to her.

I told her who she was, reminded her of her family and of Dave, and told her that I was a friend of Dave's. Then I told her she'd been in a car accident but that she would be all right. I didn't tell her about Bob. I didn't think that was fair. I reminded her of Mrs. Miller's death, though, and told her that Dave thought that someone had killed Mrs. Miller. Then I told her that Dave also thought that someone had tried to kill her.

I held her hand the entire time and carefully watched her face. She never moved her hand and her facial expression, which was completely blank, remained the same. I still wondered if she heard and understood at least some of what I'd said. I was sure I had read somewhere that people in a coma are sometimes at least partially aware of what's going on around them.

I stayed a little while longer and then I left. As I was leaving the hospital building, I saw Joe pull into a parking space. I intended to avoid him but I couldn't do it. He saw me before I had a chance to get away. At first, he didn't seem to recognize me. But when he did, he wrinkled his brow and gave me an angry look.

"What are you doing here?" he said.

My face got really red but I decided I might as well lie anyway. Maybe he would believe me.

"I was visiting a friend," I said.

He gave me a disgusted look. "You were visiting my aunt Sheila," he said. "What I want to know is why."

"I don't know," I said. "I just wanted to see how she was doing. And I'd never met her, you know. I wanted to see what she looked like."

Joe twisted up his mouth. "What for?" he said.

"I don't know," I said, sounding like he was getting on my nerves (which he was).

"Why don't you just stay away from my family?" he said.

"We're just trying to help," I said in a gentle voice. "Really we are. And you could be a big help too, if you wanted to."

He frowned at me but looked a little interested. "How?" he said with a wary expression.

"Aren't you an expert at car repairs?" I said.

A little smile formed at one corner of his mouth. "Yeah, sure. What do you want to know?" he said.

"Alicia said her parents' car has had bad brakes for quite a long time. She borrows the car when they're on vacations and that's how she noticed it."

Joe waved one of his hands at me. "Alicia doesn't know what she's talking about," he said.

"That's why I'm asking you," I said. "Did you take a look at the brakes on the day your grandmother died?"

Joe frowned but didn't answer.

"Dave was there the day your grandmother died. He said you and your mother came to visit and that Alicia asked you to look at the brakes on that car. Her parents were in Hawaii that time."

Joe was still frowning but then his face lit up. "I think you're right," he said. "I do remember that. She had me come outside and check them out."

"Was anything wrong with them?" I asked.

"Not from what I could see. I checked the brake fluid level and it was fine. When she still insisted they weren't working, I told her to have my uncle bring it in when they got back, and I'd put it on the lift so I could get a good look at the brake lines."

"Did he ever do it?" I said.

Joe squinted a little and thought for a few moments. "No, I don't think he did. But he's had it in since and I've checked everything over. The brakes were just fine."

"Can you remember the last time he brought it in?" I said.

"Maybe three months," Joe said. "Four at the most."

"Do you think it's possible something could have gone wrong with the brakes in the meantime?" I said.

"I don't see that it matters," Joe said. "Everyone knows they were tampered with. It was obvious from what the cops said. Whoever did it didn't even try to hide the fact that they were doing it on purpose."

"I know," I said, "and I think that's a little strange."

"Why's it strange?" Joe asked.

"Because you'd think they'd want to make it look like an accident so that no one would investigate it."

"Unless they were sure they'd never get caught," Joe said.

"But how could they be sure of that?" I asked.

"Seems to me it would have to be someone who thought that no one would ever suspect them in a million years. Now if you're asking me who that might be, I haven't the slightest idea. I fix cars, remember. I ain't no detective."

I smiled at him as he walked away. Then I started thinking about Sheila and Bob again and how no one in their right mind would suspect them.

# CHAPTER 9

Dave got to my house at six o'clock just as I was eating my supper. He was half an hour early.

"Did you eat?" I asked him, knowing the answer was no.

"Uh, no, I didn't, now that you mention it," he said.

I smiled. "You like stuffed green peppers, don't you?" I asked.

"I love them," he said with a grin. "Especially yours."

I ran my hand through his hair on my way to get him a plate. "You keep that up and you'll make someone a good husband someday."

He grunted and I laughed. Dave isn't exactly fond of the topic of marriage. He was married once for about eighteen months. Her name was Brenda and I think he actually loved her or believed that he did. He was only nineteen and she was at least twenty-five. He got her pregnant, agreed to marry her, and did the best he could to support her and their little boy. He was really good to her too, even though she was pretty mean to him. But then she left with Bobby and never came back. She never said good-bye and Dave gave up looking for them after about six months. He was never the same about women after that.

He only goes out with people I know he doesn't really like, not deep down. He gets only so close and then he ends it. He explains to them that he doesn't think it's working out, that it's his problem and not theirs, and he says good-bye. I sort of admire him for that. And he's pretty honest with them from the beginning. I keep telling him, though, that women never really believe that beginning stuff. They're too used to hearing it. And once they fall in love, it doesn't matter anyway. They just hang on for dear life.

\*     \*     \*

Patricia lived on 43rd Street, right in the center of a block of row homes. She looked surprised to see Dave but I don't think she minded. She asked us into the kitchen, which was on the second level. We sat at her kitchen table and watched quietly as she made us instant coffee and set out a plate of Fig Newtons. She made a cup for herself and sat down. Then she looked from Dave to me.

"What do you want to ask me?" she said to me.

I took a deep breath. I opened my mouth and closed it again. Then I looked at Dave and he gave me an impatient look. I looked back at Patricia.

"Is there any way you would agree to let us see a copy of your grandmother's will?" I said.

Patricia moved her head back a bit. "What for?" she said.

"We want to see who the beneficiaries are," I said.

"And what they were given," Dave added.

Patricia sighed and looked into her cup. Then she got up from the table and left the room. Dave raised his eyebrows and gave me a little smile.

Patricia came back with the will and handed it to me. I read through it and handed it to Dave.

"Who's Alfred?" Dave asked.

"He was my brother," Patricia said, "and Angie's father, so his share went to Angie, as you can see."

"So you, Bob, and Angie each got a third of the major part of what she had," I said.

Patricia nodded. "We each got a third of the money. Her property and belongings will be sold and those proceeds will also be divided equally."

"And Frederick was your uncle, right?" Dave said. "Your father's brother?"

"That's right," Patricia said, "but we hardly saw him. He was sort of strange."

"Yeah, Angie told us," I said. "So what's this elephant thing your mother left him?"

Patricia rolled her eyes. "It's a table made out of a log and wrapped in elephant skin," she said. "It's the ugliest thing you ever saw. I think she gave it to him as a joke."

"Did he show up when the will was read?" I said.

"No," Patricia said. "Would you show up for something like that?"

"Do you think your mother's lawyer found him?" I said.

"I doubt it," Patricia said. "No one has heard from him in years. Mother used to tell Angie that she wrote to him, though, and that they'd always kept in touch. But Angie says she used to imagine all kinds of crazy things."

"Why is that so crazy?" Dave asked. The look on his face and his tone of voice were both pretty defensive.

"Because she couldn't have known where he was," Patricia said.

"Angie told us that all of your mother's money came from your father's side of the family," I said. "Is that true?"

Patricia laughed. "It's definitely true," she said. "No one on my mother's side of the family had a cent. When we were young, they were always begging her for money."

I frowned. "I could swear Angie said your mother didn't have any relatives on her side," I said.

"Well, she doesn't anymore," Patricia said. "But she did when we were kids. She had a sister who never married and died of cancer when she was thirty-five. And both of my grandparents have been dead for years, of course."

"So all of this money was inherited by your mother from your father." I'd gotten the answer to my next question from Angie, but I wanted to see what Patricia would say. "Where did your father get it?" I asked.

Patricia laughed but it was one of those short little laughs that indicate annoyance.

"I'm sorry to be so nosy," I said. "The reason I'm asking is because of Frederick. I'm wondering if Frederick might have any reason to believe that he had a right to the money your mother got from your father."

"Oh," Patricia said in a surprised voice. "I don't know why he would. When my grandparents died, they left my father and my uncle a fair amount of money and they each got an equal amount. It wasn't a great fortune, though. The only difference is, my father had the sense to use it wisely and my uncle didn't. My uncle never had any sense at all according to my father. They each had the same chances in life, but my father ended up pretty happy and successful. My uncle just made it through from one day to the next. He never really did anything and he never really tried. For all I know he's still doing next to nothing."

"Would you know him if you saw him?" I asked her.

"Well, sure. At least I guess I would."

"How old were you the last time you saw him?" Dave asked.

"I might have been around eighteen," she said.

"So he could have changed an awful lot," Dave said. "Don't you think?"

"Yeah, I suppose you're right. I guess I might not recognize him. Why? You don't think he was at the funeral or the viewing, do you?"

"Who knows?" Dave said. "We're just throwing out ideas. Can you remember what he looked like?"

Patricia laughed. "All I can remember about him is that he smelled awful. He smoked cigars, and his clothes and hair smelled even when he wasn't smoking. It used to make me sick when he tried to kiss me."

"You wouldn't have a picture of him, would you?" Dave said.

"No," she said, "I don't. Look, I really think you're wasting your time on this. I can't believe my uncle even knows about any of this. And why would he care after all these years? He never showed any interest in me or Bob or Alfred. He's not going to suddenly show up for Bob's funeral."

"Patricia," I said, "we have one more thing we want to ask you."

She looked at me and waited for me to continue.

"Why didn't you and Joseph see your mother for such

a long time? Somebody told me it was a lot of years."

"Who told you that?" Patricia said.

I looked at Dave. "I can't remember," I said. "How long was it?"

Patricia let out a deep breath and stared at the floor. She didn't say anything for close to a minute. I was about to try again when she looked up.

"I hadn't seen or talked to her in almost fifteen years," Patricia said.

"Why?" I asked in a kind voice.

Patricia had a pained expression on her face. "Because she broke up my marriage," she said.

My eyebrows went up. "How did she do that?" I asked.

Patricia breathed in and out a few times and her eyes glistened. She took a deep breath and said, "My own mother paid my husband to leave me and my little boy. Joe was only five years old at the time."

"Oh, my gosh!" I said. "But why? Why would she do that?"

"She hated him," Patricia said. "She hated him from the first time she set eyes on him. She never even gave him a chance. She just said he was no-good trash, and she told me to get rid of him."

I gave her a sympathetic smile and let out a big sigh. "My mother was the same way with me," I said. "She hated every guy I was ever with. She said they all reminded her of my father."

Patricia laughed and a few tears flowed down her cheeks. Then her smile disappeared and more tears followed the first. "I really loved Eddie. That's what she didn't understand. I didn't care if he was no good or whatever she thought he was. I loved him and she took him away from me."

I put my hand on her arm. "I'm sorry," I said. "I really am."

Patricia smiled at me and wiped her face with a tissue she took from her pocket. "How about you?" she said. "You ever been married?"

"No," I said with a laugh. "I guess I think my mother was right. I'm too afraid I'll end up with someone like my dad."

"Do you still see your dad?" she asked.

I swallowed hard. "I never saw him," I said. "Never met the guy as far as I know."

"How about your mom?" she asked.

"I haven't seen her in over fifteen years."

Patricia laughed. "Well, don't sweat it," she said. "I wish I'd never bothered. It wasn't worth the effort. I'd always been able to tell myself she'd be glad to see me if I'd ever visit her and that maybe she'd even apologize after all those years. But she wasn't glad and she didn't apologize. Instead, she acted like I was the one who'd done something wrong."

"Then why did you come to see her on the day she died?" Dave asked calmly.

# CHAPTER
## 10

Patricia gave Dave a strange look. "Just what are you implying?" she said.

"I'm not implying anything," Dave said. "I'm just wondering. When was the last time you saw her before that day?"

Patricia looked straight into Dave's eyes. "I already told you," she said. "It was almost fifteen years ago."

"Then why did you come on that day?" Dave asked.

"The fact that it was the day she died had nothing to do with it," Patricia said. "How was I to know she'd die that night?" She looked truly upset.

"But why did you choose that day?" I said. "That's what we're wondering. It seems like such a coincidence."

"Well, it is a coincidence in a way," Patricia said. "Alicia had been telling me for the longest time that Mother was in poor health and that we really should come to see her.

Alicia said she understood how I felt, but she didn't want me to feel guilty after it was too late to do anything. I paid no attention to her at first but she got me thinking. I remembered how sorry I felt after my father died. I hadn't told him something I'd always wanted to tell him. It wasn't anything special. Well, maybe it was. It was important to me, anyway. But then he died one night unexpectedly, and I never got to tell him. I never got over that, and that's what got me to go see Mother."

I smiled at her. "Well, then I'm glad Alicia asked you to do it," I said. "Now you'll never feel that way about your mother."

Patricia looked almost amused. "It should be pretty obvious that I never got things straightened out with her on that one visit," she said. "It would have taken years and even then it probably never would have happened. Things that happen in families never really get fixed, if you want my opinion. They just get glossed over or kept out of sight."

I sighed and looked away. My own experience hadn't been much different so I didn't have anything useful to say.

"As I told you, she wasn't glad to see me anyway," Patricia said. "Not even Joe. And he was only a little kid last time she saw him. She thought we were after her money. I never expected she'd be giving me anything in the first place."

"So you were surprised when she threatened to take you out of her will?" Dave asked.

"How'd you know about that?" she said.

"I was there," Dave said. "I heard most of what happened. Everyone was yelling so loud it was hard to miss out on anything."

Patricia laughed. "It was a real scene," she said. "Mother

tried to hit me with her hot water bottle, but she didn't have the strength to really throw it."

"What did you think when she threatened to take you out of the will?" I said.

"I thought she was joking," Patricia said. "I assumed she'd done that years ago."

"So you didn't take the threat seriously?" Dave asked.

"Not at all," Patricia said. She looked confused. "Why?"

"Never mind," Dave said. "I just think I should warn you that if the police start looking into her murder, they might think it means something."

"Like I had a motive to kill her before she had a chance to change her mind," Patricia said in a calm voice.

"Exactly," Dave said.

"I can see how someone might see it that way. But I didn't do it and I'm not worried about it. The way I see it, if they start looking into her death, they'll end up finding the real murderer."

"Either that, or we'll find him first," I said.

Patricia looked amused but didn't say anything insulting. I appreciated that.

On the drive back home I asked Dave if he believed her.

"She seemed like she was telling the truth," he said. "But I don't think that means a thing. Lots of people lie and you'd never know it even if they told you they were doing it. They look so honest you just think they're kidding."

"I suppose," I said.

"What I'm wondering," Dave said, "is if any of them were in desperate need of money and possibly real fast."

"Well, I don't know how we're going to find that out," I said. "I wish we knew some other people who know each one of the people we suspect. Then we could question *those* people about the ones we suspect."

Dave smiled. "Maybe we should follow each of them around for a while. See what they do in their spare time."

I got a big grin on my face. "Yeah," I said with a lot of energy. "Who should we follow first?"

"Joe," I said before Dave had a chance to answer. "Let's follow Joe. We can hang around the place where he works and then follow him when he leaves. But we'll stay behind enough so he doesn't notice."

Dave shook his head and gave me a worried look. "I was only joking," he said. "I think you're starting to take this business too seriously. Just calm down a bit. We're going to figure this thing out. Don't worry."

Now I was really annoyed. "I want to follow him," I said in a loud voice. "If you don't want to come, you don't have to."

I could see Dave tighten his jaw. "I don't want you doing something like that alone," he said. He was acting as if he had a right to tell me what to do, which is something I really hate.

"It could get dangerous," he added, "and I want to be there in case something happens."

I didn't say anything for several minutes. Then, when I was a little calmer, I said, "I plan to follow him after he gets off work tomorrow. You are welcome to come along. Do you want to come?"

"You don't even know what time he gets off," Dave said. "You don't even know where he works."

"I do know where he works," I said. "I got it from Bob and Sheila's Rolodex."

Dave turned to me with a startled look.

"It was right after the accident when I came to the house with you," I said.

"Well, you still don't know what time he gets off," Dave muttered.

"I'll find out," I said.

Dave's jaw clenched again. "I was going out tomorrow night."

"Oh, well," I said.

He sucked in his cheeks. "Fine. I can go out the next night. Find out when he gets off. I'd ask Alicia if I were you. She's the least likely to tip him off."

I nodded and said, "Uh-huh."

"Then I'll pick you up at your place."

We were both silent the rest of the way home. He dropped me off and said a quick, unfriendly good-bye, and I went in the house.

It was almost five-thirty, so I dialed Alicia's number. Then I quickly hung up. I decided to try Farrell's Auto Body instead. I was pretty sure that Joe wouldn't answer since he was only a mechanic.

I dialed the number and a gruff, older voice said, "Auto Body, Frank here."

I took a deep breath. "Could you tell me what time Joe Bertram gets off work tonight?" I asked.

"Six-thirty," he said and he hung up.

I called Dave after I knew I'd given him enough time to get home and gave him the news. He agreed to pick me up at six-fifteen.

Dave was here at six o'clock the next day, early as always, but he didn't give me his usual warm smile so he didn't get my usual one back. We parked across from Farrell's Auto Body and waited until we caught sight of

Joe. Joe walked around from the front of an old car he was working on and removed a rear tire. He did something to it that took less than ten minutes and put it back on. Then he got in, backed it out, and parked it in a space off to one side.

He went back into the garage for about another ten minutes. When he came out, he got in his own car (a pale blue something-or-other) and drove away. He made a left and we could still see him when he got to the end of the street. There were no trees and no houses so nothing was really in the way. As soon as he turned right, we followed him.

"Hurry up or you'll lose him," I said to Dave. "We can't even see him anymore."

"The important thing is that he doesn't see us," Dave said. "And it's still light out. Just calm down. I'm not going to lose him. And if I do it's not a big deal. We'll just try again some other day."

We could see him a block and a half down as soon as we turned the corner, but he was at a red light so we had time to catch up. Dave went slow enough to keep some distance between us, though, because we would have ended up right behind him.

After the light, Joe just kept going straight. Four blocks later, he parked on the street, got out, and went into a run-down old house with a pot of pansies on the stoop. I couldn't imagine Joe putting them there and I assumed it must have been Patricia. I opened my purse and pulled out the sheet of paper with the addresses and phone numbers I'd gotten from the Rolodex. This was Joe's place, all right.

At that point, I was still having fun. There was a certain thrill to following someone and staking out his house. But more than two hours later, when he still hadn't come out and I'd had to go to the bathroom for at least an hour, I'd had enough. I was just about to admit to Dave that I couldn't take any more when Joe came back out.

I ducked down in my seat. "There he is," I said.

"I see that," said Dave. His tone of voice was still pretty sarcastic. I almost said something about it, but it wasn't the time to start a fight. So I gritted my teeth and kept quiet.

Dave waited until Joe was at the end of the second block before he started his car. He stayed two blocks behind him for the next four blocks, but then Joe made a right.

"Hurry up," I said. "We're going to lose him."

Dave glared at me but he did pick up speed. When we finally made the same turn that Joe had made, we could barely make him out. It had gotten pretty dark by then and it was hard to identify Joe's car by its color. Luckily, there was very little traffic and we got within three blocks of him before he made his next turn. When we made the turn ourselves, he was nowhere in sight.

"I can't believe this," I said. "He's driving too fast. We lost him."

"Just hang on," Dave said. He picked up his speed but looked right and left at every intersection. We finally saw him only three blocks down.

"There he is," Dave said, and I let out a breath and realized I'd been holding it for almost a minute. After that, Dave kept up with Joe, as hard as it was. It felt like we drove for miles and we ended up in an area I wasn't familiar with.

"I don't like this," Dave was saying. "I don't like this at all."

I didn't know what he meant by that, but I didn't want to ask him just then. I was too caught up in what we were doing and too nervous and scared. It was almost completely dark by then and it was hard to see things clearly.

Joe had slowed down a few blocks back, but he didn't show any signs of stopping. We drove a few more blocks and then Joe made a slow left, another slow left, and another. Then he went through the whole routine again three times and we were following him all the way. I couldn't understand how he could possibly have missed us. It had to be so obvious.

But he was looking for something or someone, so his mind was on something else. When two men in their mid-twenties came out of a doorway, Joe stopped and the men approached his car. They came toward him as if they had all the time in the world, got in the backseat, and were still there when Dave drove right by and kept on going.

When we were several blocks away, Dave let out a big sigh.

"What's the matter?" I said.

"Bad memories," he said. "You know how you feel when you go in a bar?"

"Yeah?"

"That's how I feel being back in this neighborhood. Same feeling. Exactly."

I wrinkled my brow. "What do you mean?" I said. "Why? What was going on back there?"

"Joe was buying drugs from those guys," he said. "And chances are if he's buying down here, he's got a pretty bad habit. This is dangerous territory. When I said I didn't want you going alone, I wasn't even *thinking* of something like this."

I sighed and suddenly felt very safe because I was with Dave. I felt protected and secure. It was a good, comforting feeling.

# CHAPTER 11

The next morning I had to be at a flea market by eight. Dave had promised to move my things in his truck and help me set up. But we had to stop by the Miller house first to get his tools which he had left there the night before. When we arrived, Alicia was there.

Dave knocked and Alicia answered the door. "What are you doing here?" she said to me more than to Dave.

Dave explained. Then he said, "What are you doing here so early?"

"I wanted to go visit my mother after work and bring her some different clothes," Alicia said. "I know it sounds silly since she's not even awake, but I feel like she'd want something else to wear once in a while."

"I think you're probably right," I said. "That's a nice idea."

"What do you do?" Dave said.

Alicia frowned at him.

"For a living, I mean."

"Oh," she said. "I'm a secretary. But it's just part-time and the hours are always different."

"I like that kind of job," I said. "Not having everything the same every day makes it less of a drag."

"Yeah," she said. "Right."

Dave looked at his watch and then at me. "Do we have a few minutes?" he asked me.

"Sure," I said. "But I don't want to get there too late."

"Don't worry, we won't," he said.

"Alicia," he said then. "How about you? Do you have a little time? I want to ask you a couple of questions about Joe."

Alicia perched on the arm of the couch. "Sure," she said. "Go ahead. I don't have to be at work until nine."

Dave took in a breath and let it out. "We followed him yesterday," he said.

Alicia's mouth dropped open.

"We were just trying to get an idea of what he did after work," I told her as if that were a perfectly normal thing for us to do.

Alicia looked at me like I was crazy.

"Forget all that," Dave said to me in an impatient voice. Then he looked at Alicia. "How much time do you spend with Joe and your aunt Patricia?" he said.

"Plenty," she said. "It's not like we're together all the time but I see them pretty often."

"How much time do you spend with just Joe?" Dave said. "Alone, I mean."

Alicia gave Dave a really weird look and then looked

at me as if she were asking for some sort of explanation.

"We just want to know how much you know about his private life," I said.

"Oh," she said, but she still looked confused. "Well, I know he has a girlfriend named Brenda. I've seen her a few times. She's pretty cool. I like her."

"Does he spend a lot of time with her?" Dave said.

"I don't know," Alicia said with an irritated look. "I doubt it. He's not all that serious about her. She's just a girlfriend. He's always got someone around. Of course, they usually drop him after a few months."

"They usually drop him?" I said. "Why?"

Both Alicia and Dave gave me funny looks. Can I help it if romance interests me?

"I think it's because he never takes them anywhere," Alicia said. "But why are you asking me all this? I don't see why any of this is important."

"It isn't," Dave said as he glared at me. "What I'm wondering is if you know anything about his drug use."

Alicia's eyes opened wide. "How'd you know about that?" she said.

"Like I told you, we followed him last night. He made a purchase."

"Oh," Alicia said. Then she put on a sort of disappointed look and didn't say anything for a while.

"I thought he had quit that," was the next thing she said.

"What made you think that?" Dave asked.

"He got caught dealing last year, and I thought it scared him enough that he finally wised up."

"What happened when he got caught?"

"They put him on probation. That was the other

reason I figured he'd quit. If he gets caught again, he'll be in a lot more trouble than the last time. And the other thing is it just cost him too much to buy. That's why he started dealing to begin with. It was the only way he could afford to pay for the drugs."

"How do you think he's paying for them now?" I said.

Alicia shrugged. "Either he's dealing again or he's getting it from somewhere else."

After Dave got his tools and we were back in the truck, I said, "So what do you think?"

"About what?" Dave said.

"Do you think Joe could have killed his grandmother so that his mother would inherit all that money so he could buy drugs with it?"

Dave squinted at me. "But how would he get the money away from his mother?" he said. "She wasn't just going to hand it over to him."

"Maybe she'd always promised him a portion of her inheritance as long as he was a certain age."

"Assuming she even knew she'd be getting one," Dave said. "According to her, she didn't expect anything from Mrs. Miller."

"So she says," I answered back.

I looked out the window. We were going through one of the bleaker sections of Camden. At least every third house had boards nailed over the windows and doors, some of the roofs were caved in, and abandoned cars with almost everything missing were parked along the street. There were a lot of empty lots where condemned houses had been torn down. Small children who were too young to be without their parents were playing with sticks and stones and whatever junk they could find. There was trash everywhere. I looked over at Dave but he was just staring straight ahead. Neither of us has talked about leaving Camden for almost twenty years, but when we were kids we used to talk about it all the time. We both stayed and I'm glad we did. I'm not sure why, though. Maybe it's just because it's my home. It's funny how being home can feel good even when it has a lot of unhappy memories.

As Dave was helping me unload the truck, I started talking about Alicia. "How do you think she affords all those expensive clothes and jewelry and that brand new Camaro on a part-time secretary's salary?" I asked him.

He gave me a surprised look. "Bob and Sheila," he said as if it were as obvious as could be. "They're loaded."

"But isn't that only since Mrs. Miller died?"

"They do have a lot more money since she died, but they had plenty to start with," he said. "Remember, Mrs. Miller was always giving them money. I'd hear her doing it. She was always writing out checks to Sheila for one thing or another."

"So she wasn't only giving them money to fix up the house?"

Dave thought for a moment. "I guess I don't really know the answer to that. All I know is, they were always getting money for the house, and most of the time it was Mrs. Miller who was paying me. She'd write out the check directly to me. I assume that if she did that with me she probably did that with the other workers too. So the checks to Sheila were probably for something else."

"But what?" I said. "Did you ever hear them talk about spending money on anything else?"

"It wasn't so much that I heard them talking," Dave said. "It was more what I saw. Sheila would come home from work with shopping bags full of who-knows-what almost every day. She had to be shopping on her lunch hour or something. And a lot of times, when Alicia would come over, Sheila would have some expensive piece of jewelry for her. And Alicia acted like she just expected it, so it must have happened pretty often. That's the way I look at it, anyway. I really don't see how Alicia could afford all those things with the job she has."

"So you think Mrs. Miller was paying for all this stuff either directly or indirectly?" I said.

"She had to be," Dave said. "Bob was just a truck driver and Sheila's a nurse. How much could they be making?"

# CHAPTER
## 12

$D$ave came back at the end of the day and loaded what I hadn't sold into his truck.

"Hey, you didn't do bad," he said. "Not bad at all."

I grinned at him. "I know," I said. "It was a pretty good day. I think part of the trick is knowing where you can sell what, and at what price."

Dave looked impressed and I felt warm all over. His approval means more to me than I like to admit so when I get it, it sure feels good. When I don't get it, of course, it feels just awful.

"What do you say we go and wait for Joe to get off work again?" he said.

"What for?" I said.

"To have a little talk," Dave said. "I'd like to just ask him straight out. I don't know how else we're going to find out."

I wasn't so sure about that. It almost felt like cheating. But what the heck. "Okay," I said.

We parked in the same place as we had the day before. But this time, when Joe left the lot, Dave pulled right out and honked his horn. Joe made some sort of rude remark before he realized who we were. Then he looked surprised and nervous at the same time. Dave waved for him to pull over to the side of the road. When Dave made no move to get out of the truck, Joe got out of his car and walked over. He tried to smile in a casual way, but I could tell he was having a hard time doing it.

"What's up?" he said.

"Do you have a few minutes to talk?" Dave said.

"Sure, I guess. What's on your mind?"

"Care to stop for something to eat with us?" Dave asked him.

Joe heaved a heavy sigh. "Sure," he said. "I guess I could do that."

"Hop in," Dave said.

Joe got in the backseat and I turned partly around to smile at him. He was moving his feet around and looking from side to side. "You hungry?" I said. (What else was I supposed to say?)

Joe looked at me for just a moment and then looked outside again. He couldn't seem to sit still. He was acting like a little kid who was afraid he wasn't going to make it to the bathroom on time.

"Huh? Oh, yeah. Sure," he said.

I sighed and turned around. Luckily, there's a small diner just two blocks from the body shop, and Dave was already pulling into the lot. We got out without saying a word to each other, grabbed some menus on the way in, and took the farthest table from the door. After a waitress came and took our orders, Dave said, "Joe," and Joe jumped.

Dave shook his head. "I don't know what the hell you're so afraid of, man," Dave said. "We don't mean you any harm."

Joe's shoulders relaxed a little, but he was still moving around like he had bugs all over him.

"Joe," Dave said again. "We followed you last night."

I said, "Oh, brother," and Joe put his head in his hands.

"Don't get so upset," Dave said quietly. "We're not the police. We're not going to turn you in. That's not what we're here for. All we want to know about is the money."

Joe looked up and creased his forehead. "What money?" he said.

"We know that your mother inherited a lot of money from your grandmother and that you probably knew about it before your grandmother died."

"I didn't know anything about that," Joe said. "I didn't know my grandma had any money until after she died. In fact, I thought she was already dead."

"Why'd you think that?" I said.

"Because that's what my mom told me when I was a little kid. I never knew about any money."

"But you came to visit your grandmother," I said.

"That was later," Joe said. "I only found out about her a couple of months before that. Alicia told me. She said my grandmother was still alive, and I should meet her before it was too late. I told her I didn't care. Why should I want to meet her now after all those years?"

"Didn't you ask your mom about her?" I said.

Joe tightened his jaw. "Yeah," he muttered. "I asked her but she wouldn't talk about it at first. Finally, I got it out of her but it took me a while. I couldn't believe my old man walked out on us all because my grandmother paid him to do it. What a scumbag he must have been. I hope I never set eyes on him again as long as I live."

"I don't blame you," I said, and Joe looked at me as if he could tell I meant it.

"But then how did you and your mom ever come to visit your grandmother?" Dave asked.

"My mom finally decided she wanted to go and she asked me to come along. She said it was important to her. What was I supposed to do?"

"When she threatened to take your mother out of the will, what did you think?" Dave said.

"I didn't think anything about it," Joe said. "I didn't even know she had any money. There she was in this hospital bed living in my aunt Sheila's house. I figured she couldn't even afford to live on her own."

"And your mom never said anything about the money?"

"Not a word," Joe said. "I never knew until after the funeral."

"Has she told you how much it is?" Dave asked.

Joe laughed. "It's funny you should ask that. She hasn't told me. She just says it's quite a bit and that she's going to set up a trust fund for me. I can't have anything until I get my act together."

"Meaning the drugs," Dave said.

"Right," Joe said.

"So what's holding you back, man?"

Joe looked at Dave. "It ain't that easy. You ever try to shake something like this?"

Dave gave him a look I'd seen before. "Been there," he said. Then he pulled one of his business cards out of his back pocket. "When you're ready, call me. I can tell you where to get help."

Joe shoved the card in his pocket. He didn't look like he planned to use it.

"But don't call until you're ready," Dave said in a stern voice. "It takes guts to quit."

Joe clenched his teeth and looked at the table.

After we finished eating, we dropped Joe at his car and headed for my house. "So, you going out tonight?" I asked Dave. I hadn't forgotten that he had planned to do it the night before and had cancelled because I had insisted on following Joe.

"Naw, I don't think so," he said. "What are you doing?"

"Nothing," I said. "I was just going to get a little work done and maybe watch a movie."

"Want to go see a movie?" Dave said.

I was so surprised that he'd asked that I didn't answer at first.

"Never mind," he said in a voice that sounded as if he felt rejected. "Just thought I'd ask."

"No, I'd like to," I said. "I really would. I was just trying to think if I knew of any movies I'd like to see."

He turned and gave me a big smile. "We'll go get a newspaper and find out. There has to be something playing we'd both like to see. And maybe we could go out for ice cream afterwards. That food I ordered was awful."

I laughed. "Yeah, so was mine." It really wasn't, but I was too nervous to know what else to say. I felt like I was going on a date with Dave. That was something we'd never done. I told myself over and over, just so I'd know how to act, that we weren't doing it that night, either.

# CHAPTER 13

The next morning, I got a big surprise. Dave called me at ten A.M.

"Sheila came out of her coma," he said.

I gasped. "Are you serious?" I said. "Is she all right? Is she talking?"

"Yes to all three," Dave said.

"When did you find out?"

"Last night," he said. "There was a message on my machine when I got home. I would have called you then, but it was so late I thought it could wait until morning."

"Who called you?" I asked.

"Angie," he said. "I talked to her this morning. She hadn't seen Sheila yet, but she's going over this morning. She'll let me know how she's doing."

I could hardly stand it, I was so excited. Sheila might

be able to tell us all kinds of things that no one else could. But then I suddenly remembered something.

"I wonder if anyone has told her about Bob yet," I said.

"Angie's going to tell her when she sees her," he said in a sad voice. "I asked her if it wouldn't be better to wait awhile, but she said she thought it would be better to get it over with. She'll be asking for him, first thing, anyway."

"Yeah, that's true," I said. "Well, I'll be home all day. Let me know what happens, okay?"

"I'll call you as soon as I hear anything," Dave said.

I waited all day for him to call, or at least it felt that way. I had trouble keeping my mind on my work so I cleaned instead and I really hate cleaning.

Dave called at four-thirty. "Hi," he said. "How are you doing?"

I rolled my eyes. "Dave, what happened?" I said. "Did Angie talk to Sheila? Did she tell her about Bob? What did she say?"

"I haven't heard from her," he said.

I groaned.

"Don't worry," he said. "I'll call her later."

"Okay," I said. "Let me know as soon as you hear. *Please.*"

I made myself some supper even though it was early, because I had forgotten to eat lunch. Then I went through the same crazy waiting thing I had gone through all day. Finally I gave up and called Dave.

"I was just going to call you," he said. "Why don't you come on over? Angie's on her way."

"I'll be right there," I said.

I still don't know why I was so excited. I don't know what I expected Angie to have learned from Sheila so early after coming out of the coma. But she was there when I arrived, and I had to work pretty hard to settle myself down.

"Have you seen Sheila?" I managed to ask Angie in a calm voice.

"Yes," she said with a wide grin. "You know, I don't think I really believed it until I actually saw her. I just couldn't quite see her awake. But she is and she's just fine."

I smiled. Then I frowned. "Did you tell her about Bob?" I said.

Angie winced. "Yes," she said. "She took it very hard too. I knew she would. They were so close."

"Did you ask her anything about the accident?" I said.

"No."

"Did she say anything to you about it?"

Angie shook her head. "No," she said. "And I wouldn't have wanted her to be reminded of that right now. I'm sure it would be a very frightening memory."

"Do you think they'd allow us to see her?" Dave asked.

"What do you want to see her for?" she said.

"We're trying to find out who tried to kill her," he said. "And we're also trying to find out who killed your grandmother. I promise we'll try our best not to get her upset. But the sooner we talk to her the better."

"Only relatives are allowed in," Angie said.

"Then we'll just have to say we're relatives," I said. "It worked for me the first time."

Both Dave and Angie stared at me. "The first time?" they both said at once.

I could feel myself blush.

"I went to see her one day," I said.

"Why?" Dave said with a look that made me blush even more.

"I don't know," I snapped back. "I just wanted to see what she looked like. And I wanted to tell her she'd be all right."

Dave rolled his eyes and Angie just glared.

"So, anyway," I said, trying to ignore them, "would you mind telling us what she did say?"

Angie gave me an annoyed look. "She barely said anything at all. Alicia was there and we were just asking her if she needed anything. She wanted to know how long she'd been in the coma. The usual sort of questions you'd expect from someone in her situation. She didn't say anything revealing, believe me."

"How's Alicia doing?" Dave asked.

Angie paused just a moment before she answered. "Fine," she said. "She's thrilled, of course. She had just about given up hope, you know."

"Angie," Dave said, "would you mind coming with us to see her tonight? You can tell the hospital that we're relatives. They already know you, so they'll trust you."

Angie hesitated for a moment. "Only if you promise not to upset her," she said. "If you start asking her questions that I think are bothering her, I'll have you both kicked out of there. Do you understand?"

"Yes," Dave said, and I nodded.

The three of us went to dinner first, since neither Dave nor Angie had eaten. I had a cup of coffee while they ate. I kept watching them chew and wishing they'd move faster. I wanted to talk to Sheila and I wanted to do it yesterday.

When we got to her room, she had her eyes closed and I let out a groan without meaning to. Sheila quickly opened her eyes and looked toward us. "Angie," she said with a slight smile. Then she squinted at Dave. "Dave?" she said.

"Hi, Sheila," Dave said. He sat on the edge of the bed and took hold of her hand. After talking to her for a few moments, he introduced me as a friend. I smiled and said hello, and she smiled back.

Dave asked her how she was feeling and if she was up to answering a few questions.

"You don't have to if you don't want to," Angie cut in.

Sheila waved her hand at Angie.

"What's going on here?" Alicia said from behind us. We all turned to find her standing in the doorway.

"What are you doing here?" she said to me and Dave. "Only relatives are allowed to visit. I'm calling the staff."

"No," Sheila said. She said it so sharply that Alicia stopped where she was. She held her breath for several moments and then let it out. Her face turned a deep shade of pink.

"Mother," Alicia said, "I'm sure you're not feeling well enough for all these visitors. I really think you should get some rest."

Sheila tried to laugh but it came out as a weak sort of gurgle. "All I've been doing lately is resting," she said. "It's time I did something else. Why don't you take a walk, Alicia? And take Angie with you. I'd like to talk to these people for a few minutes."

Alicia's face was bright red at that point. Angie didn't look pleased, either, but she took Alicia's arm and guided her out of the room.

"Shut the door," Sheila whispered to Dave. "I want this to be a private conversation."

Dave closed the door after looking down the hallway and waiting several moments. When he came back and sat on the edge of the bed again, Sheila looked at him with a very serious expression.

"I want to talk to you about the accident," she said.

I held my breath and Dave said, "Go ahead. I'm listening."

"I don't think it was an accident at all," she said. "I think someone meant to kill us."

# CHAPTER 14

"That's what . . ." I started to say, but Dave stopped me by putting his hand on my arm.

"Why do you think that?" he asked Sheila.

"Because Bob couldn't get the brakes to work," she said. "They didn't work at all, but we had used that car the day before and they were perfectly fine."

"Did you ever have trouble with the brakes before?" Dave asked.

"Never," Sheila said. "Not in the whole time we owned that car, and it was almost fifteen years old."

"Did Alicia tell you she'd had trouble with the brakes?" I said.

Sheila frowned at me. "No, of course not," she said. "Why do you ask?"

"She told us that she had some trouble with them. She used the car while you were on vacation."

Sheila frowned again and stared across the room. "That's right, she did," she said. "Thank goodness, she wasn't hurt."

"But she never said anything to you about the brakes?" Dave asked.

"No," Sheila said. Then she paused for a few moments. "Of course, she wouldn't be likely to tell *me* about it. She'd tell Bob. It was his car. I never drove it."

"What kind of car do you have?" I asked Sheila.

"I have a Honda Accord," Sheila said.

"What year?"

"Nineteen ninety-eight," she said.

"Did you ever use it to go to church?"

"No, we always took Bob's Buick. Bob always insisted on driving. You know how it is."

I nodded and stared out the window. I could see Dave looking at me out of the corner of my eye, but then he turned back to Sheila.

"Sheila," he said, "do you have any reason to suspect anyone in particular of trying to kill you and Bob?"

Before Sheila had a chance to answer, Angie and Alicia came back into the room. As soon as they walked in, Sheila said, "Alicia, did you tell your father about the trouble you had with the brakes on his car? Did you tell him after we got back from Jamaica?"

Alicia looked at her mother for a moment before she answered. "Yes, I did tell him," she said. "But you shouldn't be thinking about the accident right now. You're just going to upset yourself." She gave both me and Dave a dirty look.

"I just wanted to be sure you told him," Sheila said. "Did he say he'd have them looked at?"

"Yes," Alicia said. She was about to add something when Sheila broke in.

"He must not have had a chance to do it, though. We were only back two days before the accident happened."

"That's right," Alicia said. "You were. And it was Saturday morning that I told him because you got home so late on Friday night."

"Yes," Sheila said, "that's right."

Dave and I looked at each other. Alicia and Angie each took a chair and placed it close to Sheila's bed. It was clear they were there to stay.

Dave and I stood up. "We'll let you three have some time to yourselves," Dave said. Then he looked at Sheila. "Sheila, I'm so glad to have you back with us."

Sheila smiled a grateful smile. I told her I was glad to have met her, and she smiled at me too.

After Dave dropped me off at home, I made myself a cup of coffee and started making notes about the Millers. I included everything I could remember hearing about or thinking. Then I read them over and put them away. I had made notes when we solved the other two murders and it seemed to help a lot.

The next morning, I decided to see if I could get some time alone with Sheila without Angie or Sheila being there. I called Dave and asked if he wanted to come along. He almost said no because he wanted to get to work, but then he changed his mind.

"I did have a lot more that I wanted to ask her but I didn't want to do it in front of Angie and Sheila," he said.

"Do you think either of them will be there?" I said.

"It's possible," Dave said, "but we'll just have to take our chances."

Dave picked me up and we drove there in his truck. He was talking to me about Marla when we got to the hospital. We were both so lost in what we were talking about that we almost missed seeing Gus walk through the front door. I was the one who saw him first.

"Hey, isn't that Gus?" I said.

Dave looked toward the door just as Gus was opening it. His profile was to us so we could get a pretty good look at him.

"It sure is," Dave said. "I wonder what the hell he's doing here."

"Maybe we should wait until he comes out again," I said.

"No," Dave said. "I want to know who he's here to see. It's possible it's someone other than Sheila, but it would be a pretty big coincidence, don't you think?"

"I guess so," I said.

"Let's go," Dave said. "Maybe we can sneak up on him and hear something of what he says to her."

We took our time going in and signing our names in the register. Sure enough, Gus's name was there right before ours. We walked very slowly and quietly toward Sheila's room. When we were about three feet from the door, Dave put his hand on my arm and we stopped. We could hear voices but they were too quiet for us to make out what was being said.

We'd been standing there for ten minutes when I started to get impatient. I tugged on Dave's arm and pointed toward the door. He gave me an irritated look and shook his head. I was just about to say something when Gus came out and nearly ran right into us.

"Well, I'll be damned," Gus said. He sounded surprised but not the least bit angry.

Dave led him down the hall away from Sheila's room.

"Gus, what are you doing here?" Dave asked him. Dave looked Gus directly in the eye and watched his face as he waited for him to answer.

"Visiting Sheila, of course. Same as you, I expect."

Dave took a deep breath. "Gus, you barely know these people. You were at Bob's viewing and his funeral. Now you're visiting Sheila in the hospital. But the first time you even met them was the day you came to tile their bathroom. Why the special interest in their lives?"

"Seems I could ask the same of you," Gus said.

Dave paused for a moment. "You're right," he said. "I'll tell you what. If I explain to you why I'm so interested, you explain to me why you are. Fair?"

Gus turned his head to one side and winked at me. "Fair," he said. I smiled at him. There was something about him that I liked but I wasn't sure what it was.

"The police think someone tried to kill Sheila and Bob, as you already know," Dave said. "And I have thought all along that there was something very fishy about Mrs. Miller's death."

Gus creased his brow. "You think the old woman was murdered?" he said.

"I thought so when she died, but I'm more convinced than ever after what happened to Sheila and Bob. I'm just trying to find out what happened. I got pretty close to Mrs. Miller while I was making those shelves. I just want to do what I can."

Gus nodded. "Well, boy, I think it's a fine thing you're doing for the Millers. I just know they appreciate your kindness."

Dave was about to respond when Gus held up his hand.

"Now I'll keep my part of the bargain. I'm Edward's brother," he said.

"Who's Edward?" Dave asked with a frown.

"Now, I never told you I'd tell you who Edward was," Gus said as he walked away. "Maybe you can get Sheila to tell you that."

Dave started to go after him and I stopped him. "Let's just ask Sheila," I said. "I'm sure she'll tell us."

Dave shrugged and we walked into Sheila's room.

# CHAPTER
## 15

"Who's Edward?" Dave asked Sheila as soon as we stepped into the room.

Sheila jumped.

"I'm sorry," Dave said. "I didn't mean to startle you."

Sheila just looked at us and didn't answer.

"Sheila, how well do you know Gus?" I asked her.

"Gus?" she said. Then she smiled. "Oh, you must mean Frederick."

I stared at her. "You don't mean Bob's uncle, do you?"

Sheila laughed. "He certainly took me by surprise. I couldn't imagine why one of the tile men would be coming to visit me. Remember when we had the bathrooms done the month after Bob's mother died?" Sheila said to Dave.

"Yes," Dave said.

"Well, I didn't recognize him when he walked in here, but I knew he looked familiar. And then it came to me. When I asked him what he was doing here, he told me who he really was."

"So then Edward must have been Bob's father," I said.

"That's right," Sheila said.

"And Gus is Edward's brother and Bob's uncle."

"Right. Except that his name is really Frederick. He was just using the name Gus so we wouldn't know who he was."

"But didn't Bob recognize him?" Dave asked.

"I guess not," Sheila said. "He certainly never said anything to me about it. Of course, come to think of it, I'm not sure Bob ever saw him. Or if he did, it might have been only once or twice and he probably wouldn't have gotten a good look at him."

"Did he tell you why he was working in your house?" I said.

"It was purely by chance. He knew it was our house and when he was assigned to the job, he tried to get out of it but his boss wouldn't hear of it."

"How'd he know it was your house?" Dave asked.

"He claims he and Mother had been keeping in touch all these years. Off and on, anyway. And that was why he didn't show up for the reading of the will. He knew what he was getting."

"How did he know that?" I said.

"Mother told him," Sheila said.

"Do you think he was angry about it?"

Sheila thought for a few moments. "Well, no. At least, he didn't seem to be. He claimed it was a joke between the two of them. See, he and Bob's father inherited an equal amount of money when they were quite young and Frederick didn't manage his well. Edward did and was quite well off when he died. That's where Bob's mother got all her money."

"But Frederick used up all of his and is doing nothing but laying tile for people?" I asked.

Sheila frowned. "Well, I don't really know about that," she said. "He's done so many odd jobs all his life in different places. He can get a job doing just about any kind of handiwork, especially if it's on a temporary basis. I think that's what he did in this case."

"Did he say why he never told Bob who he was?"

"No," Sheila said. "He didn't say anything about that. And I didn't think to ask. If he comes back, I'll make sure I do."

"Did he tell you where he could be reached?" Dave asked.

"No," Sheila said, "he didn't."

I sighed and looked at Dave. I felt guilty because I'd told him not to bother going after Gus as he was leaving. I was so sure we could learn everything we needed from Sheila.

Dave gave me a little smile and looked back at Sheila. "Sheila," he said, "we didn't actually come here to talk about Gus—I mean Frederick. We want to talk about something we didn't get a chance to talk about last night."

"Okay," Sheila said with a wary look.

Dave took a deep breath and let it out. "I think Mrs. Miller was murdered," he said as he watched Sheila's face. "I don't think she died a natural death."

Sheila stared at Dave with her mouth open. "But she died from a diabetic coma," she said. "She ate those cookies. She was always doing things like that. That's why we had Angie there."

"I know," Dave said in a comforting voice. "I understand that. But I think someone arranged for it to happen the way it did."

"What do you mean?" Sheila said. "Arranged what? How?"

Sheila looked genuinely horrified to me. I was beginning to doubt that she could possibly be guilty.

"I think someone who knew her weaknesses put those cookies where she could easily reach them. And I think the person who did it knew that she'd eat the cookies and that she wouldn't give herself a shot of insulin. They were counting on her going into a diabetic coma."

Sheila was shaking her head with a look of disbelief on her face. "But what if she didn't eat them?" she said. "Or what if she did take the insulin? Or what if she didn't and she woke up? Then what?"

Dave shrugged. "It wouldn't have mattered," he said. "No one would have been the wiser. The killer had nothing to lose by trying. If it didn't work the first time, he or she could always try again."

Sheila gasped and stared out the window, shaking her head. "I just can't believe it," she said. "Who would do such a thing? And why?"

"Someone who knew her habits and medical problems," Dave said. "And someone who probably wanted or needed her money."

Sheila just stared at Dave with tears in her eyes. "But that means it would have to be one of us," she said.

I gave her an understanding look. "Well, you did all inherit quite a lot from her," I said.

"Yes," she said quietly. "We did. But we all got the same amount and none of us was in desperate need for the money."

"Are you sure about that?" Dave said.

Sheila wiped a tear from her cheek and looked out the window. "Well, I guess I can't be *sure*," she said. "But as far as I know, no one did."

"How often did you see Joe or Patricia?" I asked.

Sheila made a straight line with her mouth. "We never heard a word from them after Bob's mother came to live with us," she said. "It was like we'd fallen off the face of the earth. I could hardly believe it. We were always having dinner at our place or theirs before that."

"Do you think Patricia held it against Bob and you for taking Mrs. Miller in?" Dave asked.

"I know she did," Sheila said. "She told me so herself. She said it was just as if I was supporting what she did to Patricia all those years ago. I told her that was the most ridiculous thing I'd ever heard. We were just taking care of someone who couldn't care for herself properly. But she wouldn't listen to me. Patricia never did listen to anyone."

"You're talking about Mrs. Miller paying Patricia's husband to leave her?" I said.

"Now where did you hear that from?" she said.

"Joe told us," I said. "He said he thought his grandmother was dead until Alicia convinced him and his mother to come and visit because she was doing so badly."

"Alicia did that?" Sheila said with a smile.

I nodded.

"Well, that was very kind of her."

"But Joe said he didn't know about Mrs. Miller until Alicia told him. And when he asked his mother about it, that's when she told him the story about his father," Dave said.

"Are you saying it isn't true?" I asked Sheila.

Sheila sighed. "No, I guess it is true when you get right down to it. But Patricia should have been grateful. She was better off. Anyone could see that. Eddie was no good and he beat her nearly every day they were together. Her mother was just trying to help her. For all we know, she probably saved Patricia's life."

"But Patricia never saw it that way," I said.

"No, she didn't," Sheila said. "And that's why they weren't on speaking terms. It happened when Joe was only a young boy. He was too small to protect himself if Eddie went after him. Mother was protecting him too, you know, but Patricia couldn't see that either."

"Do you think Joe remembers his father?" I said.

"I know he does," Sheila said. "He remembers him leaving and he never knew why."

"Until a couple of months before his grandmother's death," Dave added.

# CHAPTER
## 16

"We have to find Gus," Dave said under his breath as soon as we were a few feet from Sheila's hospital room.

"Frederick," I said.

"Whatever," he said. Then he wrinkled his brow. "Actually, you might have something there. What if he goes by the name Frederick instead of Gus most of the time?"

"We'll just have to try both ways," I said.

"I know the company they work for," Dave said. "I'll try that first. If he doesn't work there anymore, they may know where he is."

"Or maybe Gerry will know," I added.

We stopped at a gas station that had a working phone booth (not easy to find). Dave dialed information and got the number for Martin Tile. Gus still worked there, but he and Gerry were out on a job. Dave had to leave his number and a message because the man who answered the phone refused to page either of them.

"Well, at least we know Gus—I mean Frederick—is still working for Martin Tile. That makes things a lot easier," Dave said.

It was Gerry who called Dave back later that night.

"They room together," Dave told me. "They live three blocks from my house, on Amsterdam."

I laughed. "Should we stake him out and pounce on him when he gets home from work tomorrow night?"

"We don't have to," Dave said. "He's there right now. I'll pick you up and we'll go right over."

"Won't Gerry tip him off?"

"I offered him money not to," Dave said.

"You're kidding," I said. "How much?"

"Never mind," Dave said. "It didn't take much."

We were there in ten minutes. It was a large old house that had obviously been divided into rooms for rent. Gus and Gerry lived on the first floor at the end of the hall. The door was partly open but Dave knocked anyway. Gerry answered.

"Well, Dave," he said in a voice that was too loud. "And Annie, isn't it? What brings you here?"

I rolled my eyes but Dave went along with the act. "We just came to pay a little visit," Dave said. "We were hoping to talk to Gus."

"Well, you're lucky you caught him," Gerry said in the same loud and cheery voice. "He's in the kitchen having a bowl of soup."

The kitchen was only a few feet away, it turned out, so there was no question that Gus knew we were there. He didn't seem to be bothered by it, though. When we walked into the room, he was at the kitchen table, calmly eating his soup.

"Gus," Dave said in a flat tone.

Gus didn't look up.

"Or should I call you Frederick?"

Now he looked up, at Dave and then at me. Then he put his head down again and went right on eating.

Dave took a seat at the table, right next to Gus. I sat a little farther away.

"What we were wondering," Dave said, "was why you pretended to be someone else when you came to work at the Miller house."

Gus ignored him.

"I'd pay attention, *Frederick*," Dave said, "because there's a murder or two involved here. Not to mention one attempted murder."

Gus put down his spoon and looked at Dave. Dave stared right back at him.

"I'm not involved in any murder and you know it," Gus (or Frederick) said.

"I don't know any such thing."

"You have no evidence against me for anything," Frederick said.

"But your actions are awful suspicious, wouldn't you agree?" Dave said.

"What actions?" Frederick growled.

"To start with, why didn't you let the Millers know who you were when you were at the house working?" Dave said.

Frederick let out a sigh. "That job took me by surprise,"

he said. "What was I going to say? I tried to get out of it with the boss, but he wouldn't hear of it and I couldn't tell him why. They know me as Gus at Martin Tile too. I've been going by that name for years now."

"How did you know it was their house when you were told about the job?" I said.

Frederick looked at me for the first time. "Because I recognized the address. I'd been keeping in touch with Amelia—that's Mrs. Miller, you know—off and on over the years. She'd send me a letter now and again, and I'd write back if I had the chance. I'm not too good in the letter-writing department, but I did my best."

I smiled at him. "Then why didn't you identify yourself when you got there?"

"Aw, shucks, lady. Bob hadn't seen me in who knows how long, and I knew he wouldn't recognize me. I didn't want them to see me like this. I was ashamed, I guess. All my life, I've sort of been known as the black sheep of the family, and here I was doing manual labor for one of my nephews."

"Were you at Mrs. Miller's funeral?" I said.

"Yeah, you bet I was there," he said. "None of them knew me then, either. I stayed in the background, mind you, and they didn't even notice me."

I looked at Dave. "Didn't you notice him at Mrs. Miller's funeral?" I asked him.

Dave frowned for a moment. "No," he said. "I hadn't met him yet. Bob and Sheila didn't have the bathrooms done until just after she died."

Dave suddenly turned to Frederick. "Do *you* have any idea who might want Bob and Sheila dead?"

Frederick shook his head. "No, I don't, young man. I certainly do not."

"What about Mrs. Miller?" I said.

"Amelia?" he said. "What on earth are you talking about?"

"Dave and I think she was murdered too," I said.

"Where in the world did you get such a notion?" he said to Dave.

Dave gave him a short explanation. Frederick listened very closely, shaking his head the whole time.

"Well, I'll be," he said. "Don't that beat all."

"Why didn't you show up for the reading of the will?" Dave said.

"Same reason I didn't tell them who I was at the house. I knew what I was getting anyhow," he added with a laugh. "I just told the lawyer I'd pick it up later."

"How did you know?" I said.

"Amelia told me. I always knew she wasn't leaving me anything to speak of and I didn't expect her to. By rights, that money belonged to her children. I had no claim to anything."

"But didn't it come from your father to begin with?" I said.

"What's that got to do with it?" Frederick said. He was a little annoyed at that question and I could tell he felt defensive.

"Well, you might have thought you were entitled to it since it came from your father instead of Amelia's side of the family."

Frederick shook his head a few times and pursed his lips. Then he cocked his head to one side. "Young lady," he said. "I could have but I didn't. When my father died, he left me and my brother Edward equal shares. But Edward always had a way about him. He knew what to do with things. He knew how to handle them and where to put them. Me, I was just the opposite. We were given equal chances, is the way I look at it. Wasn't Amelia's fault I didn't make the best of mine."

"Did you and your brother get along?" I asked.

Frederick looked sad for a moment. "We were on what you might call speaking terms. Even friendly most of the time. But I always believed that Edward was sort of ashamed of me, so I tried to keep my distance. I may have been wrong but that's just the way I saw it."

"Well, what do you think?" I asked Dave when we were on our way home. "Do you think he could have done it?"

Dave shook his head. "I don't know," he said. "I think it's kind of strange that he changed his identity, don't you?"

"Yeah, and I don't buy the reason he gave us for doing it. Even if he was ashamed of how he'd turned out compared to the rest of his family, why would he have to change his identity for other people? He hadn't seen anyone in his family for years and years, so why should his identity matter?"

Dave pursed his lips. "I see what you mean," he said. "And I was also thinking that he may have been angry at Mrs. Miller because of what she was leaving him in her will."

"But how would he have known about that ahead of time?" I said.

"She told him about it, remember? He admitted that himself. If it's true they were keeping in touch off and on, she could have told him in a letter she wrote to him."

"So you think he could have killed her out of anger? He'd have nothing to gain by that but revenge."

"People have killed for a lot less," Dave said.

"And what about Bob and Sheila?" I asked. "Why would he go after them? It wasn't like he was going to inherit the money after their deaths."

"Same reason," Dave said. "Anger or revenge. If he thought he was entitled to all that money, then he could have been angry enough at Bob and Sheila for getting it instead of him."

I frowned and looked out the window. "I don't know," I said. "There's something about that theory that just doesn't feel right. First of all, if he thought he was entitled to all the money and he killed Bob and Sheila because they got part of it, why wouldn't he also kill Patricia and Angie because they got the rest?"

Dave was silent for a few moments. "Good point," he said. "Unless he still plans to do it and hasn't gotten around to it yet."

# CHAPTER 17

The very next morning, Sheila came home from the hospital. Alicia brought her home and Dave was at the house when they arrived. As soon as he got a chance, he called me.

"That's great," I said. "How's she doing?"

"To be honest with you, she seems upset about being in the house."

"Maybe it's because she's thinking about how Bob should be there," I said.

"That's what I was thinking," Dave said. "I don't think she has any intentions of selling the place, though. She just asked me to build the deck in the back as soon as I'm finished with the kitchen cabinets."

"So, maybe she's—" I began. Dave stopped me.

"Hold on a minute," he said in a quiet voice. "I hear them arguing."

I kept silent until he spoke again.

"They were arguing about the deck," Dave said, still in the same soft voice.

"Who?" I said.

"Sheila and Alicia," he said. "Sheila was saying it was what Bob always wanted, and Alicia was saying what difference did it make now that he was dead. And then Sheila said it made a lot of difference because she wanted to do what he would have wanted as a way of remembering him."

"What does Alicia care, anyway?" I said. "It's not her house."

"I don't know," Dave said. "That's just Alicia's personality. She's always butting into everyone's business."

"So are you going to do it or not?" I said.

"Of course, I'm going to do it," Dave said. "Sheila's the boss, not Alicia."

I came by the Miller house later that afternoon with a pot of soup and some French bread for Sheila. I was pretty sure she wouldn't feel like cooking on her first day home. She gave me a really big smile.

"Annie, you are so sweet," she said. "Come on in. Dave's still here. He's in the kitchen building some cabinets for me."

Of course I knew that, but I didn't want her to know that I'd been in and out of her house ever since the accident.

When Dave saw me, he gave me a surprised smile. When he saw what I'd brought, his smile turned to one of those fond ones I like so much. "Hey, kid. How do you like my cabinets? They're almost done. What do you think?"

I stepped back and took a long look at the smooth paneled pine with beveled edges and custom knobs. I knew Dave had done everything himself. Nothing was pre-made. I shook my head and smiled.

"They're beautiful," I said in an awed voice. "Really beautiful."

He looked so touched and proud and Sheila looked more pleased than ever. She offered us both coffee, so Dave took a break and we sat down at the kitchen table.

"This is a beautiful house," I told Sheila. "Dave told me you've really been fixing it up. It looks great."

She smiled. "Thank you," she said. "I'll give you a tour later. We redid all the bathrooms and part of the basement. Dave built some beautiful wall-to-wall bookcases in the study and I'm having him build a deck next."

"Wow, that's quite a project," I said.

She shrugged a little. "I hadn't really wanted to spend so much money myself," she said. "It was Bob who wanted it more than anyone. But now that he's gone . . ." She stopped a moment and swallowed hard. "I want to finish it for him. I want to do all the things he had planned. The deck was one of the things he wanted most of all. We were just waiting for the weather to break to start it."

Sheila looked out the window into the backyard and her eyes filled with tears. "He was going to plant a garden around the deck," she said. "He had it all planned out. Which flowers would go where. He drew me a picture. It would have been so beautiful."

Alicia walked in just then. "Alicia," Sheila said, "I didn't know you were coming back. Look what Annie brought." She pointed to the pot of soup and the bread. "Wasn't that kind of her?"

Alicia barely looked at it and then let out a little grunt (or something close to a grunt). Sheila frowned and asked Alicia if she'd like coffee.

"No, thank you," Alicia said in an unfriendly voice. "I just wanted to see if you were doing all right, but I see you don't really need me."

Sheila sucked in her cheeks and held her breath before she let out a sigh. I had the impression that this was not unusual behavior on Alicia's part. Alicia just gave her mother a cool look and walked out. I said good-bye but she didn't say anything back.

Sheila was looking at the table after Alicia left. Dave and I looked at each other but neither of us knew what to say. In a moment, Sheila looked up and offered us more coffee. We both said yes right away though both of our cups were pretty full.

After she topped off our cups and sat down, I said, "Sheila, how often do Alicia and Patricia and Joe get together?"

Sheila frowned at me.

"I mean, are they pretty close? Do they spend a lot of time together?"

"Well, you know the story about Patricia and Bob's mother?" she said.

Dave and I nodded.

"And how Patricia wouldn't have anything to do with me or Bob after we brought Mother here to live with us?"

"Yes," Dave said.

"Well, despite how she felt about me and Bob, Patricia never seemed to hold it against Alicia, so they remained friendly."

"How old was Alicia when Mrs. Miller first came to live here?" Dave said.

Sheila thought for a moment. "Well, she's twenty-one now, twenty-two in a couple of months, and Mother was with us for about five years. So she was about seventeen."

"When did Alicia move out?" I asked.

Sheila laughed. "She lasted exactly one month after her eighteenth birthday. She said she couldn't stand having so many people in the house, so she rented a flat in Collingswood."

"She's a secretary, isn't she?" I said.

Sheila nodded. "She works part-time for an insurance agent in Collingswood, which is why she wanted to live there. She said it would save wear and tear on her car," Sheila added with an amused smile.

"It's a nice car," I said. "Was it a present?"

"Yes," Sheila said. "It was the only way we could get her to take her studies seriously. We promised her the car if she kept her grades up and went to secretarial school. She held out for the car *and* a pair of diamond stud earrings, if you can believe that, but she got her wish."

Sheila shook her head but the look on her face was good-natured. "She was Daddy's little girl, all right. Anything she wanted, Bob gave it to her. I used to try to tell him he was spoiling her too much, but he wouldn't listen. He said it wouldn't spoil her. It would just make her feel loved. I guess you never really know what's the right thing to do with your children. You just have to do what you think is right and hope for the best."

I wanted to get back to my intended topic so I just changed the subject without any warning. "So do you know if Joe and Alicia spend a lot of time together? Do you think they talk on a regular basis?"

Sheila wrinkled her forehead. "I really don't know," she said. "Why are you asking?"

"I'm wondering how much Joe has really told her about his drug problem or about any other trouble he may have gotten himself into."

Sheila raised her eyebrows. "Well, you'll have to ask her that," she said. "She never mentions him or Patricia to me. She knows better than that."

When I got home that afternoon, I called Alicia. She was there but she didn't sound happy to hear from me. I told her that I wanted to talk about Joe and asked if I could trust her to keep our conversation to herself. She said I could and invited me over that very same night.

# CHAPTER 18

When I arrived at Alicia's place, she was *almost* friendly and polite. At least she'd agreed to let me come, I told myself. I should just learn to be grateful for what I can get. She asked me if I wanted anything to drink and offered me wine, coffee, or soda. I told her soda would be good.

The flat she was renting was the first floor of an old house in a tree-lined neighborhood that looked peaceful and old-fashioned. I really liked it. Her furniture was much too showy for the house, though. The carpet was old and worn but she had it almost covered with an expensive-looking throw rug. The furniture was very modern. It was made of dark wood (which looked like cherry) with a lot of glass. She had crystal bowls and other sorts of decorative objects all around and modern pictures on the walls.

The kitchen was old, of course, but all of her glassware

and plates were expensive looking. Sheila was right. Alicia certainly was spoiled. She poured me a glass of lemon-lime soda in a frosty blue glass and added a slice of lime to it. She poured the same thing for herself.

Then she sat down at her Danish wood kitchen table and stared at me. It was a hard look at first, but then she softened it a bit.

"I have to tell you," she said as she leaned toward me. "Joe and I are very close. We are cousins, of course, and we're the same age so we grew up together. I hope you don't expect me to betray any confidences because I'm not going to do that."

"No, of course not," I said. "I would never ask you to do that."

I didn't know what to say after that since that was exactly what I had in mind. What did she think I was there for? I decided I'd better start with another subject and then sort of sneak Joe in, hoping she wouldn't notice.

"Do you think your aunt Patricia will start talking to your mother again now that your grandmother is gone?" I asked her.

She gave me a look with one eyebrow slightly above the other. "I'm close to Aunt Patricia too, you know."

I sighed.

"But I don't mind answering that because I've been wondering myself. As far as I'm concerned, it's about time Aunt Patricia forgot about that. It wasn't my mom who ruined her marriage anyway. It was my grandmother. I don't see why my aunt has to punish my mom for that just because Mom and Dad let Grandma live with them."

"It must have been hard on you to have her living there, though, wasn't it?"

Alicia looked at me sideways. "I didn't like it much.

But that has nothing to do with my mom and Aunt Patricia. That was a whole different thing."

"How did your grandmother ruin your aunt's marriage?" I said. "Did Joe ever tell you?" (Notice how I snuck that in? Clever, huh?)

Alicia squinted at me. "My mom told me my grandmother paid my uncle to just abandon them because he was no good. He was always getting in trouble and going to prison or something." (Notice how it didn't work?)

I nodded. "But your aunt still loved him, huh?"

"Yeah," Alicia said. "She talked about him all the time, like he was some kind of lost soul. If you ask me, just the fact that he took the money to leave them made him a no-good bum even if he hadn't done the other stuff."

"I know what you mean," I said. "But considering how your aunt felt, I can see why she hated your grandmother. I can see why Joe did too."

"Yeah," Alicia said. "I can see her point. And Joe was furious when he found out. He never knew until a few months before Grandma died."

"How did he find out?" I said.

Alicia rolled her eyes and looked out the window. "I told him," she said in a guilty-sounding voice. "I wanted him and Aunt Patricia to go see Grandma before she died. She was getting so old and they never went to see her. It just didn't seem right to me. I was hoping they could patch things up before it was too late."

"That was nice of you," I said.

Alicia turned down one corner of her mouth. "It didn't work out, though. When I finally did convince them to come, they just got in a big fight with Grandma and she threw them out. She thought they were coming because they wanted her money. She thought that they assumed she'd give them something if they came at the last minute before she died."

"But it's amazing how it practically *was* the last minute before she died," I said.

Alicia's face grew very still and she didn't say anything.

"Don't you think that's quite a coincidence?" I asked her.

Alicia looked at me for quite some time. Then she took a deep breath and let it out. "Yes," she finally said. "Of course I do. But I can't believe Aunt Patricia or Joe had anything to do with Grandma's death. Why would they kill her?"

"For money?" I said.

Alicia shook her head. "I don't think they even thought they'd be getting anything from her. In fact, we were all surprised that she left Aunt Patricia in the will. We were sure she had taken her out years ago."

"Have you talked to either of them about it? Did they tell you they were surprised?"

"Well, no," Alicia said. "But my mom and dad talked about it after the reading of the will. They said it was obvious Aunt Patricia was surprised. She couldn't even understand why she was asked to be there."

"Alicia, I already know all about Joe's drug problems and how he would need money for that. But is there any other reason that you know of that he'd need money?"

Alicia looked down at her hands for a few moments. Then she said, "This is between you and me, okay?" She looked into my eyes and waited for me to answer.

"Okay," I said.

"Joe got in some trouble a couple of years ago. He stole some money. A whole lot of it. And he's still paying it back. He has to give them practically his whole paycheck every week."

"So how does he live?" I said. "He has his own place and he's still buying drugs."

"It must be Aunt Patricia who's been helping him. Who else could it be?"

"But where do you think she'd get the money?" I said. "Does your aunt have a lot of money?"

"Not that I know of," Alicia said. "She works at Petite Sophisticate in the mall. She couldn't be making a whole lot. She's just a clerk."

"Could she have inherited it from someone else?" I said.

Alicia shook her head. "There is no one else."

"Well," I said as I stood up to leave. (I wanted her to think I had nothing else to ask.) "I guess I should be going. I've already taken up a lot of your time."

"Oh, that's all right," Alicia said as we walked through the dining room. Her dining room table was the same dark wood with a glass top.

"I really like your furniture," I said. "You have very good taste."

She grinned at me and looked around her. "Thank you," she said with a proud look. "I don't plan to stay here long, of course. This is just temporary until I find a better place. I want something a lot more modern."

She opened the door for me and was just about to say good-bye when I said, "Oh, I just remembered something I wanted to ask you. Angie told me that Joe and your aunt Patricia were out of town when your mom and dad got in the accident."

"Yes."

"Where were they?" I said.

"They were on vacation," Alicia said. "They go every year. They rent a cabin in the Poconos."

"Oh," I said as casually as I could. "And they told you where they would be?"

Alicia frowned. "Yes," she said. "Why?"

"Was that unusual or did they always tell you when they went on a vacation?"

"They always tell me," Alicia said. "That way I know where to reach them in case anything should happen."

# CHAPTER 19

"The way I see it," I said to Dave the next night, "we have to figure out who had the most to gain from all of this. We need to make a list or something."

Dave took a deep breath. "Okay," he said. "You're right. My bets are on Joe."

I got up and pulled a pad of paper from one of my drawers. "Okay," I said. "Tell me why."

"Because he has to give up almost all of his paycheck every week, he has a drug habit he can't kick, and he has regular monthly expenses. Then he suddenly finds out about this old woman he can't even remember who is responsible for making his dad leave him and his mother. He hears she has a lot of money, he needs a lot of money, and he has every reason to hate her. What better motive do you need?"

I raised my eyebrows. "I know," I said. "I can't really argue with any of that. So we'll put him down as a strong possibility." I made some notes about what Dave had said and put down my pen.

"All right," I said. "Now how about Patricia? Don't you think her motives are exactly the same as Joe's?"

Dave frowned. "Well, not exactly," he said, "but they're close. For instance, Patricia may have hated her even more than Joe did because she had a longer time to build up the hate. And it was Patricia that Mrs. Miller really hurt the most directly. On the other hand, Joe could be really furious because he was never even told about it until just recently. Patricia could've calmed down some over the years. But one of the differences is, why would Patricia need the money?"

"She may have just needed it to help Joe," I said. "Maybe she didn't think he could do it on his own and she'd have to help him because there was no one else. And she could have been thinking that it was Mrs. Miller's fault that there was no one else because she drove Joe's father away. So she may have felt perfectly justified in killing Mrs. Miller, who she hated anyway, to help Joe. And remember, she also hated Bob and Sheila because they took Mrs. Miller in."

"Sounds good to me," Dave said. "Put her down as strong possibility number two."

"I just thought of something," I said. "Joe and Patricia claim they thought Patricia wouldn't be getting any money from Mrs. Miller. In fact, Alicia said everyone always assumed that Patricia had been taken out of the will."

"Yeah, but both Patricia and Joe would have found out that wasn't true on the day they came to see her because she threatened to take Patricia out. And that was the same day Mrs. Miller was killed, which I've always thought was too much of a coincidence."

I nodded. "Yeah, Alicia said the same thing when I talked to her."

"How about Alicia?" Dave said. "As far as I'm concerned, she's a perfect suspect."

"But she loved her grandmother, and Bob and Sheila are her parents. They already give her everything she wants. She's about as spoiled as anyone could be. I don't see where she has anything to gain."

Dave shrugged. "Well, put her down anyway," he said.

He took the list from me when I was through. "Okay, so far we have Patricia and Joe and Alicia. What about Angie?"

"No motive," I said, "unless we find some reason why she desperately needed money. And from the looks of it, she didn't."

"Why do you say that?" Dave asked.

"Because she refused to take even a cent for taking care of Mrs. Miller, and that couldn't have been easy."

"Maybe she just did that to throw people off her trail," Dave said.

I sighed. "Okay," I said. "I'll put her down."

"All that's left is Frederick," Dave said. "He's dirt poor, could have resented Mrs. Miller for having the money that came from *his* father, and might have hated Bob and Sheila for inheriting part of it."

I wrote down his name with a question mark behind it.

Dave suddenly stood up and pushed in his chair. "Can we bag this for now?" he said. "I have to get going. I was supposed to pick up Marla a half hour ago."

I held my breath and didn't say a word.

"What's wrong?" Dave said.

"Nothing," I said. "What makes you think anything's wrong?"

"Because you have a really funny look on your face. The kind you get when something's bothering you but you don't want to talk about it."

I sighed. Dave knew me a little too well. I really didn't want him thinking I was jealous of Marla, so I decided to say something about her to throw him off the track.

"Have you talked to her about what we're doing?" I said. "Because if you have, I really don't think it's a good idea. I think it's better if we just keep this to ourselves until we figure it out, don't you?"

Dave smiled with one corner of his mouth. "No," he said slowly. "I haven't told her. I hardly ever talk to her about you anyway."

I really wished he hadn't said that because I couldn't help reacting. "Well, why not?" I said in an obviously hurt voice. "Why wouldn't you talk to her about me?"

He wrinkled his brow and leaned toward me. "You know, you're the one who told me years ago that I should never talk about other women when I'm with someone I'm dating. You do remember that, don't you?"

"Well, yeah," I said. "But I meant other women that you were involved with."

Dave opened his mouth to say something but then he stopped himself. Then all he said was, "Right. Whatever."

After he left, I made myself something to eat, had a few cups of decaf tea, and read over the notes I'd made. I tried to think about each person one by one. Why would each one of them do it? Why would they do it *when* they did? And why would they want both Mrs. Miller *and* Sheila and Bob dead?

Maybe they didn't. Maybe Mrs. Miller's death really was an accident. The only death that was pretty clearly murder was Bob's (and Sheila's if she had died). If the killer really did kill Mrs. Miller too, why was that death made to look natural and Bob and Sheila's intentional? I found that part hard to understand. If Mrs. Miller really had been murdered, the killer had gotten away with it so far. In fact, as far as I knew, Dave was the only one who had ever suspected that her death hadn't been natural.

So why the clumsy job with Sheila and Bob? Someone who had been so clever with Mrs. Miller could have been clever with Sheila and Bob too, couldn't they?

Could it have been two different killers? Crazier things have been known to happen.

I was so tired of thinking about it that I "bagged" it just as Dave suggested and watched television for the rest of the night. The next morning when I got up, I made a big breakfast, cleaned my house for about two hours, and was just about to get to work on some of my crafts when something suddenly occurred to me. I called Dave.

"Oh, my God," Dave said when I told him what I was thinking. "That means she's still in danger. Sheila would *have* to be killed for everything to work out."

"Have you seen any evidence that that might happen?" I said.

"Well, no, but I'm not here all of the time. Of course, neither is she."

"Right," I said. "Has Sheila said anything to you about going back to work?"

"She's going back on Monday," Dave said. "She says she feels strong enough now and there's no point in lying around the house."

"Where is she now?" I asked.

"Alicia took her grocery shopping," he said. "They'll be back in a little while."

I groaned.

"Don't worry. I'm sure it'll be all right," he said. "I'll call you later. How about if I stop by after work?"

"But don't you think we should do something now?" I said. "It could happen at any time and then it'll be too late. We'll never be able to live with ourselves if that happens."

"Maybe you're right," he said. "Why don't you come here instead? Bring another meal with you. It'll be a good excuse."

"Do you think we should warn her?" I said.

"I don't think she'd believe us if we did and it just might make it worse. She might end up saying something."

I was about to add something when Dave said he had to go. Sheila and Alicia were back from the store.

After I hung up, I rushed around the kitchen trying to figure out what to make for dinner. I hadn't gone grocery shopping for more than two weeks, so I didn't have a lot of provisions to choose from. I finally decided on a casserole make of rice, vegetables, and some chicken I had in the freezer. I thawed the chicken in the microwave, zapped it some more, and put the rice and vegetables on the stove to cook.

Then I started pacing across my kitchen floor. I was so worried about Sheila's safety I could barely think straight, although I guess I shouldn't have been so concerned. Dave was there with her, and I knew he'd protect her in case something should happen. What I really should have done was call the police, but I was afraid they wouldn't believe me. I really didn't have anything to go on. It was all suspicion at that point. I thought about warning Sheila, but I didn't think she'd believe me either. I wasn't sure I believed it myself.

When my little dinner was done, I packed it in a paper bag to keep it warm and tried to come up with an explanation that would sound believable. I didn't want to alarm Sheila and—I hate to admit it—I also didn't want to look too stupid. I knew I'd have to pretend that I didn't know Alicia was there because that would give away the fact that Dave had called me.

I pulled up in front of the house and sat for a few minutes trying to compose myself. It had been over forty-five minutes since I'd talked to Dave and everything appeared to be normal, at least from the outside. A light was on in the front room and another in the kitchen. I could see someone's shadow in the kitchen window over the sink. Alicia's car was in the driveway. I hadn't gotten out of dealing with her after all. What a treat.

I took the casserole out of the bag, walked up to the front door, and rang the bell.

# CHAPTER
## 20

"Annie," Sheila said with a mixture of surprise and pleasure. "What brings you here?" Then she spotted my casserole dish and her eyebrows went up very slightly. It was barely noticeable, but I was quite sure her expression now contained a bit of annoyance. My instinct was to explain my true reason for being there just in order to save face, but I knew I couldn't.

"I was sure you still wouldn't be feeling well," I said, trying to avoid her eyes. "So I thought I'd bring you dinner again. I made enough for three in case Dave is still here."

"Yes, Dave is still here," Sheila said, "and so is Alicia. She was planning to make dinner for me, so you've saved her the trouble," she added with a strained smile that made me blush.

I followed Sheila through the dining room and into the kitchen. Alicia was standing at the stove, stirring a pan of some sort of gravy that smelled very good. She was wearing a gold cotton sweater and matching linen slacks, gold jewelry, and a silk scarf in her hair. She also wore her usual aloof expression but this time there was a hint of a smile on her face.

"Alicia," Sheila said. "Look who's here. It's Annie and she's brought us dinner."

Alicia turned and glared at her mother. I could see her jaw tense but she kept her mouth shut. After staring at Sheila for a few moments (whose face I couldn't see) she turned to me.

"How nice of you," she said with a steely smile. Then she removed the gravy from the stove and poured it down the drain.

I heard Sheila let out a small gasp of surprise. "You could have saved that for later, dear," she said in a tense voice.

"It's not any good later. I'll make it some other time," Alicia said as she placed the pan in the sink.

Sheila's shoulders went up and down.

"Annie's a wonderful cook," Sheila said cheerfully. "What did you bring, Annie?" she said as she turned to me.

"It's just a casserole," I said, as if that weren't already obvious. "It's made with rice and fresh vegetables with a little chicken."

"It sounds delicious," Sheila said. "Doesn't it, Alicia?"

Sheila was trying so hard to act like things were perfectly normal that she was sounding more like she was having a nervous breakdown. She looked flustered and embarrassed by her daughter's behavior. I could hardly blame her.

"I'm sure it's quite lovely," Alicia said with an icy voice. "But I have things to do. Sorry I can't stay." She left the house without even saying good-bye. Again.

I was trying to act natural, but I was having a pretty hard time of it. I don't normally push myself into someone's life. In this case, though, I had good reason to believe Sheila's life was at stake. So I turned on her oven, asked her where her plates were, took care of a few things at the sink, and set the table for three.

When the casserole was heated and we were all seated at the table, I asked Sheila when she was going back to work. We talked about that for a while and made a lot of other boring small talk.

"Do you have any idea who might want to kill you and Bob *and* Mrs. Miller?" I asked her when I was tired of the small talk.

"I'm sure you asked me that before," Sheila said. "My answer is still the same. I have no idea."

"Has it ever occurred to you that your life may still be in danger?" I said.

Sheila shuddered a little. "Well, of course," she said. "The police even said as much. But no one's made an attempt on my life and I can't spend the rest of my days worrying about it. Maybe it was just an accident. I don't care what anybody says."

"Do you mean your and Bob's accident, or Mrs. Miller's death?" Dave said.

"Both," Sheila said. "No one but you has ever suspected that Mother was murdered. I think you've let your imagination run away with you. And Bob and me? Why? What could be the reason?"

"We think it was money," Dave said.

"And we think we know who did it," I said.

Dave gave me a sharp look as Sheila took a deep breath.

"But we're not going to say anything until we're absolutely sure," I added.

\*     \*     \*

Dave and I spent a good part of the next day waiting to hear the results of the test we'd asked the police to run. They almost turned us down. We had to tell them the whole story twice through before they started to take us seriously. I think it was the description of our suspect that got them most interested.

We were told that the test results wouldn't be in until at least four o'clock, so Dave went to work at the Miller house and I sat home painting plaques. At five after five, Dave called me.

"I just talked to the police," he said. "They said we were right."

"Oh, my God," I said.

"I still don't want to believe it's true," Dave said. "I mean, I thought it was true but now that I really know, I just can't believe it. You know what I mean?"

"Yeah," I said. "I know exactly what you mean."

"They're making the arrest right now," he said. "God. This is going to absolutely kill Sheila. I wish I knew her better. Maybe I'd know what to say."

"Hey. You were the one who figured it out, remember?"

"No," Dave said. "You were."

"But it was your suspicions that got us started. You . . ."

"Okay," Dave said. "We did it together. We're a pretty good team, don't you think?" he added in a really soft, liquid sort of voice.

I was glad he couldn't see the look on my face.

Alicia was furious when they found her. She screamed all the way to the police station, we were told. When they told her they'd found traces of her mother's sleeping pills in the gravy that was left in the pan that I took from Sheila's sink, they said she tried to break free of her handcuffs. She pulled so hard that the cuffs cut into her wrists. Then she complained that blood got on her dress. She was telling the police how much it cost and that they would have to buy her a new one if they couldn't get the blood out.

"I'm glad Bob isn't here to find out what she did," I said to Dave later that night. We were eating dinner at La Casa, one of our favorite restaurants. We were celebrating our victory. "Remember how Sheila told us she was always Daddy's little girl and that he gave her anything she wanted?"

"And look how she repaid him," Dave said. "It makes me sick to my stomach. How can anyone be so inhuman?"

"I think she's sick," I said. "She's greedy and spoiled and, on top of that, I think she's just plain sick. She admitted to killing Mrs. Miller so her parents would inherit the money. And then she tried to kill them so she'd get the money before they could spend it on the house or anything but her. And she planned it months in advance. She knew all those months ahead of time, when she was working on Joe and Patricia to come and visit Mrs. Miller, that she would kill her the same night they finally decided to come."

"What I don't understand," Dave said, "is why she worked so hard to make Mrs. Miller's death look natural and then fumbled her way through the other ones."

"Maybe she didn't know any better," I said. "Maybe she really thought people would think the brakes just didn't work right."

Dave laughed. "I suppose that's possible. She may not know any more about brakes than I do." Then he looked at me and shook his head. "I still don't understand how you came to the conclusion you did about the cars," he said.

"It was really all based on Alicia's vanity," I said. "Here she had this practically brand new Camaro, her mother had a new Honda, but she borrowed her father's *fifteen-year-old Buick* the last two times they went on vacation. It just didn't fit with her image or her personality, so I figured there had to be a reason. And then I remembered that both times she complained to people that the brakes didn't work, but according to Joe and Sheila, there had never been any sign of trouble with the brakes. That's when I decided she must have borrowed that car just so she could set the stage for the failed-brake accident she had planned for her parents for all those months." I shuddered and looked away.

"You really are good at this, you know that?" Dave said.

I smiled at him and he grinned back. I was actually enjoying myself even though the topic of discussion was pretty gruesome.

"Want to see a movie later?" he said as he carefully watched my face.

"Sure," I said.

I felt shy, like he was someone I hadn't known for a good half of my life. I was suddenly aware of his hands and his arms. The blond hair that covered his muscles. His short, clean nails. His watch. I looked at his face and saw that he was watching me. We looked at each other for a few seconds longer than usual and just breathed in and out.